SIMAK'S WORLD

The author of *Time is the Simplest Thing* and *All the Traps of Earth* is known to almost every SF fan in the country as one of today's leading exponents of the form. For vividness of imagination, for trenchant detail, for sheer creative *vitality*, Simak has few rivals in today's spectrum of SF writers.

"Simak is a prolific and markedly emotional writer who has become a kind of science fiction poet laureate . . .

"In 'Shadow Show,' Simak invents a kind of puppet-theatre with full audience participation, since they project all the actions from their minds; this forms a method of creating man beings

—...aps of Hell

STRANGERS
IN THE
UNIVERSE

Clifford D. Simak

A BERKLEY MEDALLION BOOK
published by
BERKLEY PUBLISHING CORPORATION

For SHELLEY AND SCOTT,
who will someday read these stories

COPYRIGHT © 1950, 1951, 1952, 1953, 1954, 1956,
BY CLIFFORD SIMAK

All rights reserved

*Published by arrangement with
Simon and Schuster, Inc.*

BERKLEY EDITION, SEPTEMBER, 1957
2nd printing, September, 1957 (Canada)
New Edition, October, 1963

This edition of STRANGERS IN THE UNIVERSE contains
7 of the 11 stories that appeared in the hardbound edition.

*BERKLEY MEDALLION BOOKS are published by
Berkley Publishing Corporation,
15 East 26th Street, New York 10, New York*

Printed in the United States of America

CONTENTS

TARGET GENERATION

THERE had been silence—for many generations. Then the silence ended.

The Mutter came at "dawn."

The Folk awoke, crouching in their beds, listening to the Mutter.

For had it not been spoken that one day would come the Mutter? And that the Mutter would be the beginning of the End?

Jon Hoff awoke, and Mary Hoff, his wife.

They were the only two within their cubicle, for they had no children. They were not yet allowed a child. Before they could have a child, before there would be room for it, the elderly Joshua must die, and knowing this they had waited for his death, guilty at their unspoken prayer that he soon must die—willing him to die so they might have a child.

The Mutter came and ran throughout the Ship. Then the bed in which Jon and Mary crouched spun upward from the floor and crashed against the wall, pinning them against the humming metal, while all the other furniture —chest and chairs and table—came crashing from floor to wall, where it came to rest, as if the wall suddenly had become the floor and the floor the wall.

The Holy Picture dangled from the ceiling, which a moment before had been the other wall, hung there for a moment, swaying in the air; then it, too, crashed downward.

In that moment the Mutter ended and there was silence once again—but not the olden silence, for although there was no sound one could reach out and pinpoint, there were many sounds—a feeling, if not a hearing, of the sounds of surging power, of old machinery stirring back to life, of an old order, long dormant, taking over once again.

Jon Hoff crawled out part way from beneath the bed, then straightened on his arms, using his back to lift the bed so his wife could crawl out, too. Free of the bed, they stood on the wall-that-had-become-a-floor and saw the litter of the furniture, which had not been theirs alone, but had been used and then passed down to them through many generations.

For there was nothing wasted; there was nothing thrown away. That was the law—or one of many laws—that you could not waste, that you could not throw away. You used everything there was, down to the last shred, of its utility. You ate only enough food—no more, no less. You drank only enough water—no more, no less. You used the same air over and over again—literally the same air. The wastes of your body went into the converter to be changed into something that you, or someone else, would use again. Even the dead—you used the dead again. And there had been many dead in the long generations from the First Beginning. In months to come, some day perhaps not too distant now, Joshua would be added to the dead, would give over his body to the converter for the benefit of his fellow-folk, would return, finally and irrevocably, the last of all that he had taken from the community, would pay the last debt of all his debts—and would give Jon and Mary the right to have a child.

For there must be a child, thought Jon, standing there amidst the wreckage—there must be a child to whom he could pass on the Letter and the Reading.

There was a law about the Reading, too. You did not read because reading was an evil art that came from the Beginning and the Folk had, in the Great Awakening, back in the dimness of Far Past, ferreted out this evil among many other evils and had said it must not be.

So it was an evil thing that he must pass on, an evil art, and yet there was the charge and pledge—the charge of his long-dead father had put upon him, the pledge that he had made. And something else as well: the nagging feeling that the law was wrong.

However, the laws were never wrong. There was a reason for them all. A reason for the way they lived and for the Ship and how the Ship had come to be and for those who peopled it.

Although, come to think of it, he might not pass the Letter on. He might be the one who would open it, for it said on the outside of the envelope that it was to be opened in emergency. And this, Jon Hoff told himself, might be emergency—when the silence had been broken by the Mutter and the floor became a wall and the wall a floor.

Now there were voices from the other cubicles, frightened voices that cried out, and other voices that shrieked with terror, and the thin, high crying of the children.

"Jon," said Mary Hoff, "that was the Mutter. The End will be coming now."

"We do not know," said Jon. "We shall have to wait and see. We do not know the End."

"They say . . ." said Mary, and Jon thought that was the way it always was.

They say. They say. They say.

It was spoken; it was not read nor written.

And he heard his dead father speaking once again; the memory of how he had spoken long ago came back.

The brain and the memory will play you false, for the memory will forget a thing and twist it. But the written word will stay forever as it was written down. It does not forget and does not change its meaning. You can depend upon the written word.

"They say," said Mary, "that the End will come swiftly when we hear the Mutter. That the stars will no longer move but will stand still in the blackness, and that is a sure sign the End is near at hand."

And, he wondered, the end of what? The end of us? The end of the Ship? The end of the stars themselves? Or, perhaps, the end of everything, of the Ship and stars and the great blackness in which the stars were spinning.

He shuddered to think of the end of the Folk or of the Ship, not so much that the Ship should end or that the Folk should end, but that the beautiful, efficient, well-balanced order in which they lived should end. For it was a marvelous thing that every function should be so ordered that there always would be enough for the Folk to live on, with never any surplus. No surplus of food or water or air, or of the Folk themselves, for you could not have a child until someone assigned against the coming of that child should die.

9

There were footsteps running in the corridors outside the cubicles and excited shouting, and suddenly there was someone pounding on the door.

"Jon! Jon!" the voice shouted. "The stars are standing still!"

"I knew it!" Mary cried. "I told you, Jon. It is as it was spoken."

Pounding on the door!

And the door was where it should have been, where a door logically should be, where you could walk straight out of it to the corridor instead of climbing the now useless ladder that ran ridiculously to it from the wall-that-used-to-be-the-floor.

Why didn't I think of that before? he asked himself. Why didn't I see that it was poor planning to climb to a door that opened in the ceiling?

Maybe, he thought—maybe this is the way it should have been all the time. Maybe the way it had been before was wrong. As the laws might well be wrong.

"I'm coming, Joe," said Jon.

He strode to the door and opened it, and he saw that what had been the wall of the corridor was now the floor and that many doors were opening into it directly from the cubicles and that folks were running up and down the corridor, and he thought: We can take down the ladders now, since we have no use for them. We can feed them into the converter and that will give us the margin that we never have.

Joe gripped him by the arm. "Come with me," he said.

They went to one of the topsy-turvy observation blisters. The stars were standing still.

Exactly as it had been spoken, the stars were still.

It was a frightening thing, for now you could see that the stars were not simply spinning lights that seemed to move against the flatness of a dead-black curtain, but that they were hanging in an emptiness that took the pit out of your stomach and made you gasp and clutch the metal of the ports, fighting to keep your balance, fighting off the light-headedness that came upon you as you stared into a gulf you could not understand.

10

There were no games that "day," there were no hikes, there was no revelry in the amusement lounge.

There were knots of frightened people talking. There was praying in the chapel where hung the largest of the Holy Pictures, showing the Tree and the Flowers and the River and the House far off, with a Sky that had clouds in it and a Wind you could not see, but only knew was there. There was a picking up and a straightening up of the cubicles in preparation for a "night" of sleeping and a rehanging once again of the Holy Pictures that were the prized possession of each cubicle. There was a taking down of ladders.

Mary Hoff rescued the Holy Picture from the debris on the floor and Jon stood one of the chairs against the wall and hung it upon the wall-that-once-had-been-the-floor and wondered how it happened that each of the Holy Pictures was a little different from all the others. And it was the first time he had ever wondered that.

The Hoffs' Holy Picture had a Tree in it, too, and there were Sheep beneath the Tree and a Fence and Brook, and in the corner of the picture there were some tiny Flowers, and, of course, the Grass that ran up to the Sky.

After he had hung the picture and Mary had gone off to another cubicle to talk in horror-stricken, old-wife fashion with some of the other women, Jon went down the corridor, strolling as casually as he could so that no one would notice him, so that no one would mark any hurry in him.

But there was hurry in him—a sudden, terrible hurry that tried to push him on like two hands against his back.

He tried to look as if he were doing nothing more than genteelly killing time. It was easy for him, for that was all he'd done his entire life, all that any of them had ever done. Except the few, the lucky or unlucky ones, whichever way you might look at it, who had the hereditary jobs—tending the hydroponic gardens * or the cattle pens or the poultry flocks.

---

* *Hydroponics is the art of growing plants in water with added chemical nutrients instead of soil. The feasibility of hydroponics has been well demonstrated in many experiments, but so far has not proved in any case I know of to be economically successful. Chemicals necessary to plant growth are carbon, oxygen, hydro-*

But most of them, thought Jon, loitering his way along, had done no more than become expert in the art of killing time. Like himself and Joe, with their endless chess games and the careful records that they kept of every move they made, of every move and game. And the hours they spent in analyzing their play from the records that they made, carefully annotating each decisive move. And why not? he asked himself—why not record and annotate the games? What else was there to do? What else?

There were no people now in the corridor and it had grown dimmer, for now there were only occasional light bulbs to drive back the darkness. Years of bulb-snatching to keep the living cubicles supplied had nearly stripped the Ship.

He came to an observation blister and ducked into it, crouching just inside of it, waiting patiently and watching back along his trail. He waited for the one who might have followed him and he knew there would be no one, but there *might be* someone and he couldn't take the chance.

No one came, and he went on again, coming to the broken-down escalator which went to the central levels, and here, once again, there was something different. Always before, as he had climbed level after level, he had steadily lost weight, lost the pull against his feet, had swum rather than walked toward the center of the Ship. But this time there was no loss of weight, this time

---

gen, nitrogen, potassium, calcium, magnesium, sulphur, phosphorus, and iron. Small quantities of boron, zinc, manganese, and copper also are required. Molybdenum is necessary in extremely minute quantities. On board a spaceship, hydroponics would be an ideal way to produce food, with the added advantage that the plant growth would aid in atmospheric engineering by absorbing carbon dioxide and releasing oxygen. In hydroponics aboard a spaceship there would be no seasons; crops would be growing all the time. Although some insect pests might exist, to start with, these probably would be eradicated after a human generation or less, so that the crops would be pest-free. The same situation would exist so far as plant disease is concerned. Once either pests or disease were eliminated within a spaceship there would be no further danger, since reinfection from other crop areas could not occur. Since there would be on board a spaceship nothing equivalent to sunlight, necessary for the growth of plants, the deficiency would have to be supplied by the use of lamps.—C. S.

there was no swimming. He trudged broken escalator after broken escalator for all the sixteen decks.

He went in darkness now, for here the bulbs were entirely gone, snatched or burned out over many years. He felt his way upward, with his hand along the guide rails, feeling the cross-draft of the corridors that plunged down the great Ship's length.

He came at last to the proper level and felt his way along until he came to the hiding place, a dispensary room with a pharmaceutical locker against one wall.

He found the proper drawer and pulled it open, and his hand went in and found the three things that he knew were there—the Letter, the Book, and a bulb.

He ran his hand along the wall until he found the outlet, and when he found it he inserted the bulb and there was light in the tiny room, light upon the dust that lay across the floor and along the counter tops, light upon the wash basin and the sink, the empty cabinets with their idly open doors.

He laid the Letter face up beneath the light and read the words that were printed in block letters:

TO BE OPENED ONLY IN EMERGENCY.

He stood there for a long time, considering. There had been the Mutter. The stars were standing still.

Emergency, he thought. This is emergency.

For had it not been spoken that when the Mutter came and the stars stood still the End was near at hand?

And if the End was near at hand, then it was emergency.

He lifted the Letter in his hand and held it, hesitating. When he opened it, that would be the end of it. There would be no more handing down—no more of the Letter and the Reading. For this was the moment toward which the Letter had traveled down through time, from father to son for many generations.

Slowly he turned the Letter over and ran a thumbnail along the sealed edge, and the dry wax cracked open and the flap sprang loose.

He reached in and took the message out and spread it flat upon the counter top underneath the lamp. He read, his lips moving to form whispered words, reading as one must read who had spelled out the slow meaning of his words from an ancient dictionary:

To the son of my son many times removed:

They will have told you and by this time you may well believe that the ship is a way of life, that it started in a myth and moves toward a legend and that there is no meaning to be sought within its actuality and no purpose.

It would be fruitless for me to try to tell you the meaning or the purpose of the ship, for, while these words are true, by themselves, they will have little weight against the perversion of the truth, which by the time you read this may have reached the stature of religion.

But there is purpose in the ship, although even now, as this is written, the purpose has been lost, and as the ship plunges on its way it will remain not only lost, but buried beneath the weight of human rationalizing.

In the day that this is read there will be explanations of the ship and the people in it, but there will be no knowledge in the explanations.

To bring the ship to its destination there must be knowledge. There is a way that knowledge may be gained. I, who will be dead, whose body will have gone back into a plant long eaten, a piece of cloth long worn out, a molecule of oxygen, a pinch of fertilizer, have preserved that knowledge for you. On the second sheet of this letter are the directions for the acquiring of that knowledge.

I charge you to acquire that knowledge and to use it, that the minds and lives which launched the ship, and the others who kept it going, and those who even now reside within its walls may not have used themselves, nor dedicated themselves, in vain, that the dream of Man may not die somewhere far among the stars.

You will have learned by the time you read this, even to a greater degree than I know it today, that nothing must be wasted, nothing must be thrown away, that all resources must be guarded and husbanded against a future need.

And that the ship not reach its destination, that it not serve its purpose, would be a waste so great as to stun the imagination. It would be a terrible waste of

14

thousands of lives, the waste of knowledge and of hope.

You will not know my name, for my name by the time you read this will be gone with the hand that drives the pen, but my words will still live on and the knowledge in them and the charge.

I sign myself, your ancestor.

And there was a scrawl that Jon could not make out.

He let the Letter drop to the dust-laden counter top and words from the Letter hammered in his brain.

A ship that started in a myth and moved toward a legend. But that was wrong, the Letter said. There was a purpose and there was a destination.

A destination? What was that? The Book, he thought —the Book will tell what destination is.

With shaking hands he hauled the Book out of the drawer and opened it to *D* and followed down the columns with an unsteady finger: *desquamative, dessert, destinate, destination—*

Destination (n). The place set for the end of a journey, or to which something is sent; a place or point aimed at.

The Ship had a destination. The Ship was going somewhere. The day would come when it would reach the place that it was going. And that would be the End, of course. The Ship was going somewhere. But how? Did the Ship move?

He shook his head in disbelief. That the Ship moved was unbelievable. It was the stars, not the Ship, that moved.

There must be, he felt certain, another explanation.

He picked up the Letter's second sheet and read it through, but didn't understand it all, for his brain was tired and befuddled. He put the Letter and the Book and the bulb back in the drawer.

He closed the drawer and fled.

They had not noticed his absence in the lower level and he moved among them, trying to be one of them again, trying to pick up the old cloak of familiarity and wrap it around his sudden nakedness—but he was not one of them.

A terrible knowledge had made him not one of them—the knowledge that the Ship had a purpose and a destination—that it had started somewhere and was going somewhere and that when it got where it was going that would be the End, not of the Folk, nor of the Ship, but only of the Journey.

He went into the lounge and stood for a moment just inside the doorway. Joe was playing chess with Pete and a swift anger flared within him at the thought that Joe would play with someone else, for Joe had not played chess with anyone but him for many, many years. But the anger dropped quickly from him, and he looked at the chessmen for the first time, really saw them for the first time, and he saw that they were idle hunks of carven wood and that they had no part in this new world of the Letter and the Purpose.

George was sitting by himself playing solitaire and some of the others were playing poker with the metal counters they called "money," although why they called it money was more than anyone could tell. It was just a name, they said, as the Ship was the name for the ship and the Stars were what the stars were called. Louise and Irma were sitting in one corner listening to an old, almost worn-out recording of a song, and the shrill, pinched voice of the woman who sang screeched across the room:

"My love has gone to the stars,
He will be away for long . . ."

Jon walked into the room and George looked up from the cards. "We've been looking for you."

"I went for a walk," said Jon. "A long walk. On the center levels. It's all wrong up there. It's up, not in. You climb all the way."

"The stars have not moved all day," said George.

Joe turned his head and said, "The stars won't move again. This is as it was spoken. This is the beginning of the End."

"What is the End?" asked Jon.

"I don't know," said Joe and went back to his game.

The End, Jon thought. And none of them know what the End will be, just as they do not know what a ship is, or what money is, or the stars.

16

"We are meeting," said George. Jon nodded.

He should have known that they would meet. They'd meet for comfort and security. They'd tell the Story once again and they'd pray before the Picture. And I? he thought. And I?

He swung from the room and went out into the corridor, thinking that it might have been best if there'd been no Letter and no Book, for then he'd still be one of them and not a naked stranger standing by himself—not a man torn with wondering which was right, the Story or the Letter.

He found his cubicle and went into it. Mary was there, stretched out on the bed, with the pillows piled beneath her head and the dim bulb burning. "There you are," she said.

"I went for a walk," said Jon.

"You missed the meal," said Mary. "Here it is."

He saw it on the table and went there, drawing up a chair. "Thanks," he said.

She yawned. "It was a tiring day," she said. "Everyone was so excited. They are meeting."

There was the protein yeast, the spinach and the peas, a thick slice of bread and a bowl of soup, tasty with mushrooms and herbs. And the water bottle, with the carefully measured liquid.

He bent above the soup bowl, spooning the food into his mouth.

"You aren't excited, dear. Not like the rest."

He lifted his head and looked at her. Suddenly he wondered if he might not tell her, but thrust the thought swiftly to one side, afraid that in his longing for human understanding he finally would tell her. He must watch himself, he thought.

For the telling of it would be proclaimed heresy, the denying of the Story, of the Myth and the Legend. And once she had heard it, she, like the others, would shrink from him and he'd see the loathing in her eyes.

With himself it was different, for he had lived on the fringe of heresy for almost all his life, ever since that day his father had talked to him and told him of the Book. For the Book itself was a part of heresy.

"I have been thinking," he said, and she asked, "What is there to think about?"

17

And what she said was true, of course. There was nothing to think about. It was all explained, all neat and orderly. The Story told of the Beginning and the beginning of the End. And there was nothing, absolutely nothing for one to think about.

There had been chaos, and out of the chaos order had been born in the shape of the Ship, and outside the Ship there was chaos still. It was only within the Ship that there was order and efficiency and law—or the many laws, the waste not, want not law and all the other laws. There would be an End, but the End was something that was still a mystery, although there still was hope, for with the Ship had been born the Holy Pictures and these in themselves were a symbol of that hope, for within the picture were the symbolism values of other ordered places (bigger ships, perhaps) and all of these symbol values had come equipped with names, with Tree and Book and Sky and Clouds and other things one could not see, but knew were there, like the Wind and Sunshine.

The Beginning had been long ago, so many generations back that the stories and the tales and folklore of the mighty men and women of those long-gone ages pinched out with other shadowy men and women still misty in the background.

"I was scared at first," said Mary, "but I am scared no longer. This is the way that it was spoken, and there is nothing we can do except to know it is for the best."

He went on eating, listening to the sound of passing feet, to the sound of voices going past the door. Now there was no hurry in the feet, no terror in the voices. It hadn't taken long, he thought, for the Folk to settle down. Their ship had been turned topsy-turvy, but it was still for the best.

And he wondered if they might not be the ones who were right, after all—and the Letter wrong.

He would have liked to step to the door and hail some of those who were passing by so he could talk with them, but there was no one in the Ship (not even Mary) he could talk to.

Unless it were Joshua.

He sat eating, thinking of Joshua in the hydroponic gardens, pottering around, fussing with his plants.

As a boy, he'd gone there, along with the other boys, Joe and George and Herb and all the rest of them, Joshua then had been a man of middle age who always had a story and some sage advice and a smuggled tomato or a radish for a hungry boy. He had, Jon remembered, a soft gentle way of talking, and his eyes were honest eyes, and there was a gruff but winning friendliness about him.

It had been a long time, he realized, since he'd seen Joshua. Guilt, perhaps, he told himself.

But Joshua would be one who could understand the guilt. For once before he had understood.

It had been he and Joe, Jon remembered, who had sneaked in and stolen the tomatoes and been caught and lectured by the gardener. Joe and he had been friends ever since they had been toddlers. They had always been together. When there was devilment afoot the two of them were sure, somehow, to be in the middle of it.

Maybe Joe . . . Jon shook his head. Not Joe, he thought. Even if he was his best friend, even if they had been pals as boys, even if they had stood up for each other when they had been married, even if they had been chess partners for more than twenty years—even so, Joe was not one he could tell about this thing.

"You still are thinking, dear," said Mary.

"I'll quit," said Jon. "Tell me about your day."

She told him. What Louise had said; and what Jane had said; and how foolish Molly was. The wild rumor and the terror and the slow quieting of the terror with the realization that, whatever came, it was for the best.

"Our Belief," she said, "is a comfort, Jon, at a time like this."

"Yes," said Jon. "A great comfort, indeed."

She got up from the bed. "I'm going down to see Louise," she said. "You'll stay here?" She bent and kissed him.

"I'll walk around until meeting time," he said.

He finished his meal, drank the water slowly, savoring each drop, then went out.

He headed for the hydroponic gardens. Joshua was there, a little older, his hair a little whiter, his shuffle

19

more pronounced, but with the same kind crinkle about his eyes, the same slow smile upon his face.

And his greeting was the joke of old: "You come to steal tomatoes?"

"Not this time," said Jon.

"You and the other one."

"His name is Joe."

"I remember now. Sometimes I forget. I am getting older and sometimes I forget." His smile was quiet. "I won't take too long, lad. I won't make you and Mary wait."

"That's not so important now," said Jon.

"I was afraid that after what had happened you would not come to see me."

"It is the law," said Jon. "Neither you nor I, nor Mary, had anything to do with it. The law is right. We cannot change the law."

Joshua put out a hand and laid it on Jon's arm. "Look at the new tomatoes," he said. "They're the best I've ever grown. Just ready to be picked." He picked one, the ripest and the reddest, and handed it to Jon.

Jon rubbed the bright red fruit between his hands, feeling the smooth, warm texture of it, feeling the juice of it flow beneath the skin.

"They taste better right off the vine. Go ahead and eat it."

Jon lifted it to his mouth and set his teeth into it and caught the taste of it, the freshly picked taste, felt the soft pulp sliding down his throat.

"You were saying something, lad."

Jon shook his head.

"You have not been to see me since it happened," said Joshua. "The guilt of knowing I must die before you have a child kept you away from me. It's a hard thing, I grant—harder for you than it is for me. You would not have come except for a matter of importance."

Jon did not answer.

"Tonight," said Joshua, "you remembered you could talk to me. You used to come and talk with me often, because you remembered the talk you had with me when you were a kid."

"I broke the law," said Jon. "I came to steal tomatoes. Joe and I, and you caught us."

"I broke the law just now," said Joshua. "I gave you a tomato. It was not mine to give. It was not yours to take. But I broke the law because the law is nothing more than reason and the giving of one tomato does not harm the reason. There must be reason behind each law or there is no occasion for the law. If there is no reason, then the law is wrong."

"But to break a law is wrong."

"Listen," said Joshua. "You remember this morning?"

"Of course I do."

"Look at those tracks—the metal tracks, set deep into the metal, running up the wall."

Jon looked and saw them.

"That wall," said Joshua, "was the floor until this morning."

"But the tanks! They . . ."

"Exactly," said Joshua. "That's exactly what I thought. That's the first thing I thought when I was thrown out of bed. My tanks, I thought. All my beautiful tanks. Hanging up there on the wall. Fastened to the floor and hanging on the wall. With the water spilling out of them. With the plants dumped out of them. With the chemicals all wasted. But it didn't happen that way."

He reached out and tapped Jon on the chest.

"It didn't happen that way—not because of a certain law, but because of a certain reason. Look at the floor beneath your feet."

Jon looked down and the tracks were there, a continuation of the tracks that ran up the wall.

"The tanks are anchored to those tracks," said Joshua. "There are wheels enclosed within those tracks. When the floor changed to the wall, the tanks ran down the tracks and up the wall that became the floor and everything was all right. There was a little water spilled and some plants were damaged, but not many of them."

"It was planned," said Jon. "The Ship . . ."

"There must be reason to justify each law," Joshua told him. "There was reason here and a law as well. But the law was only a reminder not to violate the reason. If there were only reason you might forget it, or you might defy it or you might say that it had become outdated. But the law supplies authority and you follow law where you might not follow reason.

"The law said that the tracks on the wall, the old wall, that is, must be kept clear of obstacles and must be lubricated. At times we wondered why, for it seemed a useless law. But because it was a law we followed it quite blindly and so, when the Mutter came, the tracks were clear and oiled and the tanks ran up them. There was nothing in the way of their doing so, as there might have been if we'd not followed the law. For by following the law, we also followed the reason and it's the reason and not the law that counts."

"You're trying to tell me something," Jon said.

"I'm trying to tell you that we must follow each law blindly until we know the reason for it. And when we know, if we ever know, the reason and the purpose, we must then be able to judge whether the reason or the purpose is a worthy one. We must have the courage to say that it is bad, if it is bad. For if the reason is bad, then the law itself is bad, for a law is no more than a rule designed for a certain reason or to carry out a purpose."

"Purpose?"

"Certainly, lad, the purpose. For there must be some purpose. Nothing so well planned as the Ship could be without a purpose."

"The Ship itself? You think the Ship has purpose? They say . . ."

"I know what they say. Everything that happens must be for the best." He wagged his head. "There must have been a purpose, even for the Ship. Sometime, long ago, that purpose must have been plain and clear. But we've forgotten it. There must be certain facts and knowledge . . ."

"There was knowledge in the books," said Jon. "But they burned the books."

"There were certain untruths in them," said the old man. "Or what appeared to be untruths. But you cannot judge the truth until you have the facts and I doubt they had the facts. There were other reasons, other factors.

"I'm a lonely man. I have a job to do, and not many come to visit. I have not had gossip to distract me although the Ship is full of gossip. I have thought. I have done a lot of thinking. I thought about us and the Ship. I thought about the laws and the purpose of it all.

"I have wondered what makes a plant grow, why water

and chemicals are necessary to its growth. I have wondered why we must turn on the lamps for just so many hours—what is there in the lamps that helps a plant to grow? But if you forget to turn them on, the plant will start to die, so I know the lamps are needed, that the plants need, not water and chemicals alone, but the lamps as well.

"I have wondered why a tomato always grows on a tomato vine and why a cucumber always grows on a cucumber vine. You never find a tomato on a cucumber vine and there must be a reason.

"Behind even so simple a thing as the growing of tomatoes there must be a mass of reasons, certain basic facts. And we do not know these facts. We do not have the knowledge.

"I have wondered what it is that makes the lamps light up when you throw the switch.

"I have wondered what our bodies do with food. How does your body use that tomato you've just eaten? Why must we eat to live? Why must we sleep? How did we learn to talk?"

"I have never thought of all that," said Jon.

"You have never thought at all," said Joshua, "or almost not at all."

"No one does," said Jon.

"That is the trouble with the Ship," the old man told him. "No one ever thinks. They while away their time. They never dig for reasons. They never even wonder. Whatever happens must be for the best, and that's enough for them."

"I have just begun to think," said Jon.

"There was something you wanted," said the old man. "Some reason that you came."

"It doesn't matter now," said Jon. "You have answered it."

He went back, through the alleyways between the tanks, smelling the scent of green things growing, listening to the gurgle of the water running through the pumps. Back up the long corridors, with the stars shining true and steady now through the ports in the observation blisters.

Reason, Joshua had said. There is reason and a purpose. And that had been what the Letter had said, too—reason and a purpose. And as well as truths there will be

23

untruths, and one must have certain knowledge to judge a thing, to say if it is true or not.

He squared his shoulders and went on.

The meeting was well under way when he reached the chapel, and he slid in quietly through the door and found Mary there. He stood beside her and she slipped her hand in his and smiled.

"You are late," she whispered.

"Sorry," he whispered back, and then they stood there, side by side, holding hands, watching the flicker of the two great candles that flanked the massive Holy Picture.

Jon thought that never before had he seen it to such good advantage nor seen it quite so well and he knew that it was a great occasion when they burned the candles for it.

He identified the men who sat below the Picture—Joe, his friend, and Greg and Frank. And he was proud that Joe, his friend, should be one of the three who sat beneath the Picture, for you must be pious and a leader to sit beneath the Picture.

They had finished reciting the Beginning and now Joe got up and began to lead them in the Ending.

"We go toward an End. There will be certain signs that shall foretell the coming of the End, but of the End itself no one may know, for it is unrevealed . . ."

Jon felt Mary's hand tighten upon his and he returned the pressure, and in the press of hand to hand he felt the comfort of a wife and of Belief and the security of the brotherhood of all the Folk.

It was a comfort, Mary had said while he had eaten the meal she had saved for him. There is comfort in our Belief, she'd said. And what she had said was true. There was comfort in Belief, comfort in knowing that it all was planned, that it was for the best, that even in the End it would be for the best.

They needed comfort, he thought. They needed comfort more than anything. They were so alone, especially so alone since the stars had stopped their spinning and stood still, since you could stand at a port and look out into the emptiness that lay between the stars. Made more alone by the lack of purpose, by the lack of knowing,

24

although it was a comfort to know that all was for the best.

"The Mutter will come and the stars will stop their spin and they will stand naked and alone and bright in the depth of darkness, of the eternal darkness that covers everything except the Folk within the Ship. . . ."

And that was it, thought Jon. The special dispensation that gave them the comfort. The special knowing that they, of all the things there were, were sheltered and protected from eternal night. Although, he wondered, how did the special knowing come about? From what source of knowledge did it spring? From what revelation? And blamed himself for thinking as he did, for it was not seemly that he should think such things at meeting in the chapel.

He was like Joshua, he told himself. He questioned everything. He wondered about the things that he had accepted all his life, that had been accepted without question for all the generations.

He lifted his head and looked at the Holy Picture—at the Tree and the Flowers and the River and the House far off, with the Sky that had Clouds in it and Wind you could not see but knew was there.

It was a pretty thing—it was beautiful. There were colors in it he had never seen anywhere except in the Pictures. Was there a place like that? he wondered. Or was it only symbolism, only an idealization of the finest that was in the Folk, a distillation of the dreams of those shut up within the Ship?

Shut up in the Ship! He gasped that he had thought it. Shut up! Not shut up. Protected, rather. Protected and sheltered and kept from harm, set apart from all else which lay in the shadow of eternal night. He bent his head in prayer, a prayer of contriteness and self-accusation. That he should think a thing like that!

He felt Mary's hand in his and thought of the child that they would have when Joshua was dead. He thought of the chess games he had played with Joe. He thought of the long nights in the darkness with Mary at his side.

He thought of his father, and the long-dead words thundered in his brain. And the Letter that spoke of knowledge and of destination and had a word of purpose.

25

What am I to do? he asked himself. Which road am I to follow? What is the Meaning and the End?

He counted the doors and found the right one and went in. The place was thick with dust, but the light bulb still survived. Against the farther wall was the door that was mentioned in the instruction sheet enclosed within the Letter—the door with the dial built into its center. A vault, the instruction sheet had said.

He walked across the floor, leaving footprints behind him in the dust, and knelt before the door. With his shirtsleeve he wiped the dust from the lock and read the numbers there. He laid the sheet upon the floor and grasped the dial. Turn the indicator first to 6, then to 15, back to 8, then to 22 and finally to 3. He did it carefully, following the instructions, and at the final turn to 3 he heard the faint chucking sound of steel tumblers dropping into place.

He grasped the handle of the door and tugged, and the door came open slowly, because it was heavy. He went inside and thumbed the switch and the lights came on, and everything was exactly as the instruction sheet had said. There was the bed and the machine beside it and the great steel box standing in one corner.

The air was foul, but there was no dust, since the vault was not tied in with the air-conditioning system which through centuries had spread the dust through all the other rooms.

Standing there alone, in the glare of the bulb, with the bed and machine and great steel box before him, terror came upon him, a ravening terror that shook him even as he tried to stand erect and taut to keep it away from him—a swift backlash of fear garnered from the many generations of unknowing and uncaring.

Knowledge—and there was a fear of knowledge, for knowledge was an evil thing. Years ago they had decided that, the ones who made decisions for the Ship, and they had made a law against Reading and they had burned the books.

The Letter said that knowledge was a necessary thing.

And Joshua, standing beside the tomato tank, with the other tanks and their growing things about him, had said that there must be reason and that knowledge would disclose the reason.

26

But it was only the Letter and Joshua—only the two of them against all the others, only the two of them against the decision that had been made many generations back.

No, he said, talking to himself, no, not those two alone —but my father and his father before him and fathers before that, handing down the Letter and the Book and the art of Reading. And he, himself, he knew, if he had had a child, would have handed him the Letter and the Book and would have taught him how to read. He could envision it—the two of them crouched in some obscure hiding place beneath the dim glow of a bulb, slowly studying out the way that letters went together to form the words, doing a thing that was forbidden, continuing a chain of heresy that had snaked its way throughout the Folk for many generations.

And here, finally, was the end result, the bed and machine and the great steel box. Here, at last, was the thing to which it all had pointed.

He went to the bed, approaching it gingerly, as if it might be a hidden trap. He poked and prodded it and it was a bed and nothing more.

Turning from the bed to the machine he went over it carefully, checking the wiring contacts as the instructions said he should, finding the cap, finding the switches, checking on other vital points. He found two loose contact points and he tightened them, and finally, after some hesitation, he threw on the first switch, as the instructions said he should, and the red light glowed.

So he was all ready.

He climbed into the bed and took up the cap and set it on his head, twisting it securely into place. Then he lay down and reached out and snapped on the second switch and there was a lullaby.

A lullaby, a singing, a tune running in his brain and a sense of gentle rocking and of drowsiness.

Jon Hoff went to sleep.

He woke and there was knowledge.

A slow, painful groping to recognize the place, the wall without the Holy Picture, the strange machine, the strange thick door, the cap upon his head.

His hands went up and took off the cap and he held it, staring at it, and slowly he knew what it was. Bit

27

by painful bit, it all came back to him, the finding of the room, the opening of the vault, checking the machine and lying down with the cap tight upon his head.

The knowledge of where he was and why he was there—and a greater knowledge. A knowing of things he had not known before. Of frightening things.

He dropped the cap into his lap and sat stark upright, with his hands reaching out to grasp the edges of the bed.

Space! An emptiness. A mighty emptiness, filled with flaming suns that were called the stars. And across that space, across the stretches of it too vast to be measured by the mile, too great to be measured by anything but light-years, the space crossed by light in the passage of a year, sped a thing that was called a ship—not the Ship, Ship with a capital *S*, but simply a ship, one of many ships.

A ship from the planet Earth—not from the sun itself, not from the star, but from one of many planets that circled round the star.

It can't be, he told himself. It simply cannot be. The Ship can't move. There can't be space. There can't be emptiness. We can't be a single dot, a lost and wandering mote in the immensity of a universal emptiness, dwarfed by the stars that shine outside the port.

Because if that were so, then they stood for nothing. They were just casual factors in the universe. Even less than casual factors. Less than nothing. A smear of wandering, random life lost amid the countless stars.

He swung his legs off the bed and sat there, staring at the machine.

Knowledge stored in there, he thought. That's what the instruction sheet had said. Knowledge stored on spools of tape, knowledge that was drummed into the brain, that was impressed, implanted, grafted on the brain of a sleeping man.

And this was just the beginning. This was only the first lesson. This was just the start of the old dead knowledge scrapped so long ago, a knowledge stored against a day of need, a knowledge hid away. And it was his. It lay upon the spools, it lay within the cap. It was his to take and his to use—and to what purpose? For there was no

28

need to have the knowledge if there were no purpose in it.

And was it true? That was the question. Was the knowledge true? How could you know a truth? How could you recognize an untruth?

There was no way to know, of course—not yet was there a way to know the truth. Knowledge could be judged by other knowledge, and he had but little knowledge—more than anyone within the ship had had for years, yet still so little knowledge. For somewhere, he knew, there must be an explanation for the stars and for the planets that circled around the stars and for the space in which the stars were placed—and for the Ship that sped between the stars.

The Letter had said *purpose* and it had said *destination* and those were the two things he must know—the purpose and the destination.

He put the cap back in its place and went out of the vault and locked the door behind him, and he walked with a slightly surer stride, but still with the sense of guilt riding on his shoulders. For now he had broken not only the spirit, but the letter of the law—he was breaking the law for a reason and he suspected that the reason and the purpose would wipe out the law.

He went down the long flights of the escalator stairs to the lower levels.

He found Joe in the lounge, staring at the chess board with the pieces set and ready.

"Where have you been?" asked Joe. "I've been waiting for you."

"Just around," said Jon.

"This is three days," said Joe, "you've been just around." He looked at Jon quizzically.

"Remember the hell we used to raise?" he asked. "The stealing and the tricks?"

"I remember, Joe."

"You always got a funny look about you, just before we went off on one of our pranks. You have that same look now."

"I'm not up to any pranks," said Jon. "I'm not stealing anything."

"We've been friends for years," said Joe. "You've got something on your mind. . . ."

29

Looking down at him, Jon tried to see the boy, but the boy was gone. Instead was the man who sat beneath the Picture, the man who read the Ending, the pious man, the good man, a leader of the Ship's community.

He shook his head. "I'm sorry, Joe."

"I only want to help."

But if he knew, thought Jon, he wouldn't want to help. He'd look at me in horror, he'd report me to the chapel, he'd be the first to cry heresy. For it was heresy, there was no doubt of that. It was a denial of the Myth, it was a ripping away of the security of ignorance, it was a refutation of the belief that all would be for the best, it was saying they could no longer sit with folded hands and rely upon the planned order of the Ship.

"Let's play a game," he said with resolve.

"That's the way you want it, Jon?" demanded Joe.

"That's the way I want it."

"Your move," said Joe.

Jon moved his queen pawn. Joe stared at him. "You play a king's pawn game."

"I changed my mind," said Jon. "I think this opening's better."

"As you wish," said Joe.

They played. Joe won without any trouble.

At last, after days of lying on the bed and wearing the cap, of being lullabied to sleep and waking with new knowledge, Jon knew the entire story.

He knew about the Earth and how Earthmen had built the ship and sent it out to reach the stars, and he understood a little about the reaching for the stars that had driven humans to plan the ship.

He knew about the selection and the training of the crew and the careful screening that had gone into the picking of the ancestors of the colonists-to-be, the biological recommendations that had determined their mating so that when the fortieth generation should finally reach the stars they would be a hardy race, efficient and ready to deal with the problems there.

He knew about the educational setup and the books that had been intended to keep knowledge intact, and he had some slight acquaintance with the psychology involved in the entire project.

30

But something had gone wrong. Not with the ship, but with the people in it.

The books had been fed into the converter. The Myth had risen and Earth had been forgotten. The knowledge had been lost and legend had been substituted. In the span of forty generations the plan had been lost and the purpose been forgotten and the Folk lived out their lives in the sure and sane belief that they were self-contained, that the Ship was the beginning and the end, that by some divine intervention the Ship and the people in it had come into being, and that their ordered lives were directed by a worked-out plan in which everything that happened must be for the best.

They played chess and cards and listened to old music, never questioning for a moment who had invented cards or chess or who had created music. They whiled away not hours, but lives, with long gossiping, and told old stories, and swapped old yarns out of other generations. But they had no history and they did not wonder and they did not look ahead—for everything that happened would be for the best.*

For year on empty year the Ship was all they had known. Even before the first generation had died the

---

*The importance of written records as opposed to memory insofar as accuracy is desirable was pointed out many years ago by Sir George Cornewall Lewis, the British historian, who made an exhaustive study of the credibility of early Roman history. As a result of this study, Lewis arrived at the conclusion that a tradition of a past event is not transmitted orally from generation to generation with anything like accuracy of detail for more than a century, and in most instances for a considerably lesser period. Therefore, on a thousand-year flight, if written records were not kept, it is extremely likely that Earth would be forgotten or, at best, would exist only as a legend. A thousand years, in this day of multibillion financing, seems a small number and is easy to say or write, but is terribly long in actual time. The time since the invasion of England by William the Conqueror is not yet a thousand years. America was discovered by the Vikings not quite a thousand years ago, by Columbus less than half a thousand years ago. If records had not been kept of the Columbus voyage or of the Norman invasion, they would now be forgotten incidents and subject to the speculation of historian theorists. As it is, the Viking voyages to America are very imperfectly known, since only fragments of their record exist, written down many years after the event from the sagas which commemorated them.—C. S.

Earth had become a misty thing far behind, not only in time and space, but in memory as well. There was no loyalty to Earth to keep alive the memory of the Earth. There was no loyalty to the Ship, because the Ship had no need of it.

The Ship was a mother to them and they nestled in it. The Ship fed them and sheltered them and kept them safe from harm.

There was no place to go. Nothing to do. Nothing to think about. And they adapted.

Babies, Jon Hoff thought. Babies cuddling in a mother's arms. Babies prattling old storied rhymes on the nursery floor. And some of the rhymes were truer than they knew.

It had been spoken that when the Mutter came and the stars stood still the End was near at hand.

And that was true enough, for the stars had moved because the Ship was spinning on its longitudinal axis to afford artificial gravity.

But when the Ship neared the destination, it would automatically halt the spin and resume its normal flight, with things called gyroscopes taking over to provide the gravity.

Even now the Ship was plunging down toward the star and the solar system at which it had been aimed. Plunging down upon it if—and Jon Hoff sweated as he thought of it—if it had not already overshot its mark.

For the people might have changed, but the Ship did not. The Ship did not adapt. The Ship remembered when its passengers forgot. True to the taped instructions that had been fed into it more than a thousand years before, it had held its course, it had retained the purpose, it had kept its rendezvous, and even now it neared its destination.

Automatic, but not entirely automatic.

It could not establish an orbit around the target planet without the help of a human brain, without a human hand to tell it what to do. For a thousand years it might get along without its human, but in the final moment it would need him to complete its purpose.

And I, Jon Hoff told himself, I am that man.

One man. Could one man do it?

He thought about the other men. About Joe and Herb

and George and all the rest of them, and there was none of them that he could trust, no one of them to whom he could go and tell what he had done.

He held the Ship within his mind. He knew the theory and the operation, but it might take more than theory and more than operation. It might take familiarity and training. A man might have to live with a ship before he could run it. And there'd be no time for him to live with it.

He stood beside the machine that had given him the knowledge, with all the tape run through it now, with its purpose finally accomplished, as the Letter had accomplished its purpose, as Mankind and the Ship would accomplish theirs if his brain was clear and his hand was steady. And if he knew enough.

There was yet the chest standing in the corner. He would open that—and finally it would be done. All that those others could do for him would then be done and the rest would depend on him.

Moving slowly, he knelt before the chest and opened the lid.

There were rolls of paper, many rolls of it, and beneath the paper, books, dozens of books, and in one corner a glassite capsule enclosing a piece of mechanism that he knew could be nothing but a gun, although he'd never seen one.

He reached for the glassite capsule and lifted it, and beneath the capsule was an envelope with one word printed on it: KEYS.

He took the envelope and tore it open and there were two keys. The tag on one said: CONTROL ROOM; the tag on the other: ENGINE ROOM.

He put the keys in his pocket and grasped the glassite capsule. With a quick twitch, he wrenched it in two. There was a little puffing sound as the vacuum within the tube puffed out, and the gun lay in his hands.

It was not heavy, but heavy enough to give it authority. It had a look of strength about it and a look of grim cruelty, and he grasped it by the butt and lifted it and pointed, and he felt the ancient surge of vicious power—the power of Man, the killer—and he was ashamed.

He laid the gun back in the chest and drew out one of the rolls of paper. It crackled, protesting, as he gently unrolled it. It was a drawing of some sort, and he bent above it to make out what it was, worrying out the printed words that went with the lines.

He couldn't make head or tail of it, so he put it down and it rolled into a cylinder again as if it were alive.

He took out another one and unrolled it, and this time it was a plan for a section of the Ship.

Another one and another one, and they were sections of the Ship, too—the corridors and escalators, the observation blisters, the cubicles.

And finally he unrolled one that showed the Ship itself, a cross-section of it, with all the cubicles in place and the hydroponic gardens. And up in the nose the control room, and in the back the engine rooms.

He spread it out and studied it and it wasn't right, until he figured out that if you cut off the control room and the engine room it would be. And that, he told himself, was the way it should be, for someone long ago had locked both control and engine rooms to keep them safe from harm—to keep them safe from harm against this very day.

To the Folk, the engine room and control room had simply not existed, and that was why, he told himself, the blueprint had seemed wrong.

He let the blueprint roll up unaided and took out another one, and this time it was the engine room. He studied it, crinkling his brow, trying to make out what was there, and while there were certain installations he could guess at, there were many that he couldn't.

He made out the converter and wondered how the converter could be in a locked engine room when they'd used it all these years. But finally he saw that the converter had two openings, one beyond the hydroponic gardens and the other within the engine room itself.

He let go of the blueprint and it rolled up, just like all the others. He crouched there, rocking on his toes a little, staring at the blueprints, thinking: If there were any further proof needed to convince me, there lies that simple proof.

Plans and blueprints for the ship. Plans dreamed by men and drawn by human hands. A dream of stars

34

drawn on a piece of paper. No divine intervention. No myth. Just simple human planning.

He thought of the Holy Pictures and he wondered what they were. They, too—could they, too, be as wide of the mark as the story of the Myth? And if they were, it seemed a shame. For they were such a comfort. And the Belief as well. It had been a comfort, too.

He crouched in the smallness of the vault, with the machine and bed and chest, with the rolled-up blueprints at his feet, and brought up his arms across his chest and hugged himself in what was almost abject pity.

He wished that he had never started. He wished there had been no Letter. He wished that he were back again, in the ignorance and security. Back again, playing chess with Joe.

Joe said, from the doorway, "So this is where you've been hiding out."

He saw Joe's feet, planted on the floor, and he let his eyes move up, following Joe's body until he reached his face. The smile was frozen there. A half-smiled smile frozen solid on Joe's face.

"Books!" said Joe.

It was an obscene word. The way Joe said it, it was an obscene word. As if one had been caught in some unmentionable act, surprised with a dirty thought dangling naked in one's mind.

"Joe—" said Jon.

"You wouldn't tell me," said Joe. "You said you didn't want my help. I don't wonder that you didn't . . ."

"Joe, listen—"

"Sneaking off with books," said Joe.

"Look, Joe. Everything's all wrong. People like us made this ship. It is going somewhere. I know the meaning of the End . . ."

The wonder and the horror were gone from Joe's face now. It had become bleak. It was a judge's face. It towered above him and there was no mercy in it—not even any pity.

"Joe!"

Joe turned around swiftly, leaping for the door.

"Joe! Wait a minute, Joe!" But he was gone.

The sound of his feet came back, the sound of them

running along the corridor, heading for the escalator that would take him down to the living levels.

Running back and going down to cry up the pack. To send them tonguing through the entire ship hunting down Jon Hoff. And when they caught Jon Hoff . . .

When they caught Jon Hoff that would be the End for always. That would make the End the kind of unknown End that was spoken in the chapel. For there would be no other—there would never be another who would know the Meaning and the Purpose and the Destination.

And because of that, thousands of men and women would have died in vain. The sweat and genius and longing of the people who had launched the ship would have been for nothing.

It would be a terrible waste. And wasting was a crime. You must not waste. You must not throw away. And that meant human lives and dreams as well as food and water.

Jon's hand reached out and grasped the gun and his fingers tightened on it as the rage grew in him, the rage of desperation, the last-hope rage, the momentary, almost blinded madness of a man who sees the rug of life being deliberately jerked from beneath his feet.

Although it was not his life alone, but the lives of all the others—Mary's life, and Herb's and Louise's and Joshua's as well.

He was running at full tilt when he went out the door and he skidded as he made the sharp right-angle turn into the corridor. He flung himself in the direction of the escalator and in the darkness felt the treads beneath his feet, and he breathed a thankfulness for the many times he had gone from the living quarters to the center of the Ship, feeling his way in darkness. For now he was at home in the darkness and that was an advantage he had that Joe did not possess.

He hurled himself down the stairs, skidded and raced along the corridor, found the second flight—and ahead of him he heard the running, stumbling footsteps of the man who fled ahead of him.

In the next corridor, he knew, there was a single lamp, burning dimly at the end of the corridor. If he could reach the corridor in time . . .

He went down the treads, one hand on the rail to keep himself from falling, scarcely touching the treads, sliding down rather than running.

He hit the floor in a crouch, bent low, and there, outlined against the dimly burning lamp, was a running figure. He lifted the gun and pressed the button, and the gun leaped in his hands and the corridor suddenly was filled with flame.

The light blinded him for a second and he remained crouching there, and the thought ran through him: I've killed Joe, my friend.

Except it wasn't Joe. It wasn't the boy he'd grown up with. It wasn't the man who had sat opposite him at the chess board. It was not Joe, his friend. It was someone else—a man with a judge's face, a man who had run to cry up the pack, a man who would have condemned them all to the End that was unknown.

He felt somehow that he was right, but nevertheless he trembled.

His sight came back and there was a huddled blackness on the floor.

And now his hand was shaking and he crouched there without moving and felt the sickness heaving at his stomach and the weakness crawl along his body.

You must not waste.

You must not throw away.

Those were spoken laws. But there were other laws that never had been spoken because there had been no need to speak them. They had not spoken you must not steal another's wife, they had not spoken you must not bear false witness, they had not spoken you must not kill—for those were crimes that had been wiped out long before the star-ship had leaped away from Earth.

Those were the laws of decency and good taste. And he had broken one of them. He had killed a fellow man. He had killed his friend.

Except, he told himself, he was not my friend. He was an enemy—the enemy of all of us.

Jon Hoff stood erect and stopped his body's shaking. He thrust the gun into his belt and walked woodenly down the corridor toward the huddle on the floor.

The darkness made it a little easier, for he could not see what lay there as well as if it had been light. The face lay against the floor and he could not see the face. It would have been harder had the face stared up at him.

He stood there considering. In just a little while the Folk would miss Joe and would start to hunt for him. And they must not find him. They must never know. The idea of killing had long since been wiped away; there could be no suggestion of it. For if one man killed, no matter how or why, then there might be others who would kill. If one man sinned, his sinning must be hidden, for from one sinning might come other sinning, and when they reached the new world, when (and if) they reached the target planet, they would need all the inner strength, all the fellowship and fellow-security they could muster up.

He could not hide the body, for there was no hiding place but could be found. He could not feed it to the converter because he could not reach the converter. To reach it he'd have to go through the hydroponic gardens.

But no, of course, he wouldn't. There was another way to reach the converter—through the engine room.

He patted his pocket and the keys were there. He bent and grasped Joe and recoiled at the touch of the flesh, still warm. He shrank back against the metal wall and stood there, and his stomach churned and the guilt of what he'd done hammered in his head.

He thought of his father talking to him—the granite-faced old man—and he thought of the man, far back, who had written the Letter, and he thought of all the others, who had passed it on, committing heresy for the sake of truth, for the sake of knowledge and salvation.

There had been too much ventured, too much dared and braved, too many lonely nights of wondering if what one did was right, to lose it now because of squeamishness or guilt.

He walked out from the wall and grasped the body and slung it on his shoulder.

It dangled. It gurgled. Something wet and warm trickled down his back.

He gritted his teeth to keep them from chattering. And he staggered along beneath his burden, climbing the long-stilled escalators, clopping along the corridors, heading for the engine room.

At last he reached the door and laid the burden down

to fumble for the keys. He found them and selected the right one and turned it in the door, and when he pushed against the door it swung slowly open. A gust of warm air came out and slapped him in the face. Lights glowed brightly and there was a humming song of power and the whine of spinning metal.

He reached down and lifted Joe again and went in and closed the door. He stood staring down the long paths that ran between the great machines.

There was one machine that spun, and he recognized it—a gyroscope, a stabilizer hanging in its gimbals, humming to itself.

How long, he wondered, how long would it take a man to understand all there was to know about all these massive, intricate machines? How far, he wondered, have we fallen from the knowledge of a thousand years ago?

And the thing he carried dangled on his shoulder, and he heard the slow, deliberate dripping of the warm, sticky liquid splashing on the floor.

Horror and wonder—a going back. A going back through a thousand years to a knowledge that could build machines like these. A going back much farther to an instability of human emotions that would drive one man to kill another man.

I must be rid of him, Jon Hoff thought bitterly. I must be rid of him. But I never will be. When he has disappeared; when he has become something other than what he is, when the substances of him have become something else, I still shall not be rid of him. Never!

He found the converter door and braced himself in front of it. He tugged at the door. It stuck, and he jerked at it and it came free. The maw gaped, large enough to take a human body, and from behind the baffles he could hear the roaring of the power and imagined that he caught the hellish flicker of the ravening fire. He balanced the body on his shoulder and slid it off as gently as he could, feeding it to the maw. He gave it a final push and closed the door and trod hard upon the feeder mechanism.

The deed finally was done.

He reeled back from the converter's face and mopped his brow and now the burden was gone, but it still was

39

with him. As it always would be, he thought. *As it always would be.*

The footsteps came at him, and he did not swing around to face them, for he knew whose the footsteps were—the ghostly footsteps that would dog him all his life—the footsteps of guilt walking in his mind.

A voice said, "Lad, what have you done?"

Jon said, "I have killed a man. I have killed my friend." And he swung around to face the footsteps and the voice, because neither was a ghost.

Joshua said, "There was a reason for it, lad?"

"A reason," said Jon Hoff. "A reason and a purpose."

"You need a friend," Joshua said. "You need a friend, my boy."

Jon nodded. "I found the purpose of the Ship. And the destination. He found me out. He was going to denounce me. I—I—"

"You killed him."

"I thought, One life or all? I took only one life. He would have taken all."

They stood for a long moment, facing each other.

The old man said, "It is not right to take a life. It is not right nor proper."

He stood there, stumpy and stolid, against the background of the engines, but there was something vital in him, some driving force within him as there was in the engines.

"Nor is it right," he said, "to condemn the Folk to a fate that was not intended. It is not right to let a purpose go by default and ignorance."

He asked. "The purpose of the Ship? It is a good purpose?"

"I do not know," said Jon. "I can't be sure. But at least it is a purpose. A purpose, any purpose, is better than none at all." He raised his head and brushed back his hair, plastered down with sweat across his brow.

"All right," he said. "I'll go along with you. I've taken one life. I'll not take any more."

Joshua spoke slowly, gently. "No, lad. I am the one who goes along with you."

To see the great depth of the emptiness in which the stars blazed like tiny, eternal watch fires was bad enough when one looked out a blister port. To see it from the control room, where the great glass plate opened out into the very jaws of space, was something else again.

You could look down and down and there was no bottom, and you could look up or out and there was no stopping, and one moment you would swear that a certain star could be reached for and plucked, and the next moment it was so far away that your brain spun with the very thought of distance.

The stars were far.

All but one of them. And that one blazed, a flaming sun, off toward the left.

Jon Hoff flicked a glance at Joshua, and the old man's face was frozen in a mask that was disbelief and fear and something touching horror.

And, he thought, I knew. I knew what it *might* be like. I had some idea. But he had none at all.

He pulled his eyes from the vision plate and saw the banks of instruments, and his stomach seemed to turn over and his fingers were all thumbs.

No time to live with the Ship, he told himself. No time to get to know it as it really is. What must be done he must do by intellect alone, by the sketchy knowledge impressed upon his brain—a brain that was not trained or ready, that would not be trained and ready for many years.

"What are we to do?" Joshua whispered. "Lad, what are we to do?"

And Jon Hoff thought: *What are we to do?*

He walked slowly forward and mounted the steps to the chair that said NAVIGATOR on the back of it.

Slowly he hoisted himself into the chair, and it seemed that he sat on the edge of space itself, that he sat upon a precipice from which at any moment he might slip off and tumble into space.

He put his hands down carefully and gripped the chair's arms and hung on tight and fought to orient himself, to know that he sat in a navigator's chair and that in front of him were trips and buttons that he could press or trip, and that the pressing and the tripping of them would send signals to the pulsing engine room.

"That star," said Joshua. "That big one off to the left. The burning one . . ."

"All the stars are burning."

"But that one. The big one . . ."

"That's the one we headed for a thousand years ago," said Jon. And he hoped it was. He wished he could be certain that it was the one.

Even as he thought it, bells of alarm were ringing in his brain. There was something wrong. Something very wrong.

He tried to think, but space was too close to think, space was too big and empty and there was no use of thinking. One could not outwit space. One could not fight space. It was too big and cruel. Space did not care. It had no mercy in it. It did not care what happened to the ship or the people in it.

The only ones who had ever cared had been the people back on Earth who had launched the Ship, and, for a little while, the Folk who rode the Ship. And finally, he and one old man. They two against all space. The only ones who cared.

"It's bigger than the others," said Joshua. "We are closer to it."

That was what was wrong! That was what had rung the alarm within his mind. The star was far too close—it shouldn't be that close!

He wrenched his eyes from space and looked down at the control board, and all he saw was a meaningless mass of trips and levers, banks of buttons, rows of dials.

He watched the board and slowly his mind began to sort it out, to make some sense of it, the knowledge the machine had pounded into him beginning to take over. He read the dials and he got some knowledge from them. He located certain controls that he had to know about. Mathematics rose unbidden in his brain and did a nightmare dance.

It was useless, he told himself. It had been a good idea, but it hadn't worked. You couldn't educate a man by a machine. You couldn't pound into him the knowledge necessary to navigate a ship.

"I can't do it, Joshua," he cried. "It's impossible to do it."

Where were the planets? he wondered. How could he find the planets? And when he found them, if he found them, what would he do then?

The Ship was falling toward the sun.

He didn't know where to look for planets. And they were going too fast—they were going far too fast. Sweat burst out upon him, beading his brow and running down his face, dripping from his armpits.

"Take it easy, lad. Take it easy now."

He tried to take it easy, but it didn't work. He reached down and slid open the tiny drawer beneath the control panel. There was paper there and pencils. He took out a sheet of paper and a pencil. He jotted down the readings on the dials: absolute velocity; increase of velocity; distance from the star; angular approach to the star.

There were other readings, but those were the essential ones, those were the ones that counted.

And one thought rose in his brain, one thought that had been impressed upon it time after time: *To navigate a ship is not a matter of driving it toward a certain point, but of knowing where it will be at any time within the immediate future.*

He made his calculations; the mathematics struggling upward into his consciousness. He made the calculations and he made a graph and then reached out and pushed a control lever forward two notches and hoped that he was right.

"You are making it out?" Joshua asked.

Jon shook his head. "We'll know—an hour from now we'll know."

A slight increase in thrust to keep the Ship from plunging too close toward the sun. Skirting the sun and curving back, under the attraction of the sun, making a long wide loop out into space, and then back toward the sun again. That was the way it worked—that was the way he hoped it worked. That was the way the machine had told him it might work.

He sat there limp, wondering about the strange machine, wondering how much reliance you could put in tape running on a spool and a cap clamped on your head.

"We'll be here a long time," said Joshua.

Jon nodded. "I am afraid so, Joshua. It will take a long time."

"Then," the old man said, "I'll go and get some food." He started toward the door, then turned back.

"Mary?" he asked.

Jon shook his head. "Not yet. Let's leave them in peace. If we fail . . ."

"We won't fail."

Jon spoke sharply. "If we do, it's best they never know."

"You may be right," the old man said. "I'll go and get the food."

Two hours later Jon knew that the Ship would not crash the sun. It would come close, almost too close for comfort—only a million miles or so away—but the Ship's velocity would be such that it would skim past the sun and climb out into space again, pulled to one side by the attraction of the sun, fighting outward against the pull of the flaming star, dropping off its speed on the upward, outward haul.

With its flight path curved inward by the sun, it would establish an orbit—a highly dangerous orbit, for on the next swing around, left to its own devices, the ship would crash the sun.

Between the time that it passed the sun and curved inward once again he must establish control over it, but the important thing was that he had bought some time. Without the added two notches of velocity he had gained by the shoving of the lever, he was sure, the ship either would have plunged into the sun or would have established a tightening orbit about it from which even the fantastic power of the mighty engines could not have pulled it free.

He had time and he had some knowledge, and Joshua had gone to bring some food. He had time and he had to use the time. He had the knowledge, lying somewhere in his brain, planted there, and he must dig it up and put it to the job for which it was intended.

He was calmer now and a little surer of himself. And he wondered, in his own awkwardness, how the men who had launched the ship from Earth, the men who had watched and tended it before the Ignorance, could have shot so closely. Chance, perhaps, for it would have been impossible to shoot a thousand-year-long missile at a tiny target and have it hold its course—or would it have been possible?

Automatic . . . automatic . . . automatic . . . the word

44

thrummed in his brain. The single word over and over again. The ship was automatic. It ran itself, it repaired itself, it serviced itself, it held true to the target. It needed only the hand and brain of Man to tell it what to do. Do this, the hand and brain of Man would say, and the Ship would do it. That was all that was needed—the simple telling of instructions.

The problem was how to tell the Ship. What and how to tell it. And there were certain facts that haunted him about the telling of the Ship.

He got down from the navigator's chair and prowled about the room. There was a thin fine dust on everything, but when he rubbed his sleeve along the metal, the metal shone as brightly as on that day it had been installed.

He found things, and some of them he knew and recognized and some of them he didn't. But, most important, he found the telescope, and after some trials and errors, he remembered how to operate it. And now he knew how to find the planets—if this was the target star and there were any planets.

Three hours gone and Joshua had not returned. It was too long to be gone just to get some food. Jon paced up and down the room, fighting down his fears. Something had happened, something must have happened to the old man.

He went back to the telescope and began the work of running down the planets. It was hard work and purposeless at first, but bit by bit, with the handling of the instruments, the facts started drifting up into his consciousness.

He found one planet—and there was a knock upon the door. He left the telescope and strode across the room.

The corridor was full of people, and all at once they were shouting at him, shouting hateful words, and the roaring of their voices was a blast of anger and of condemnation that sent him back a step.

In front were Herb and George and behind them all the others—men and women both. He looked for Mary, but he didn't see her.

The crowd surged forward and there was hatred and loathing on their faces, and the fog of fear came out of them and struck deep into Jon Hoff.

45

His hand went down to his waistband and closed upon the gun butt and he dragged the weapon free. He tilted the gun downward and stabbed at the button, just one quick, light stab. Light bloomed out and filled the doorway, and the crowd went reeling back. The door itself was blackened and there was the smell of blistered paint.

Jon Hoff spoke evenly. "This is a gun," he said. "With it I can kill you. With it I *will* kill you if you interfere. Stand back. Go back where you came."

Herb took a forward step and stopped. "You are the one who is interfering," he declared. He took another step.

Jon brought the gun up and lined its sights on him.

"I've killed one man," he said, "and I'll kill another." And he thought, So easy to talk of killing, of taking human life. So ready to do it, now that I've killed once.

"Joe is missing," said Herb. "We have been hunting for him."

"You need to hunt no more," said Jon.

"But Joe was your friend."

"And so are you," said Jon. "But the purpose is too big for friendship. You're with me or against me. There is no middle ground."

"We'll read you out of chapel."

"You'll read me out of chapel," said Jon, mocking him.

"We'll exile you to the central ship."

"We've been exiled all our lives," said Jon. "For many generations. And we didn't even know it. We didn't know, I tell you. And because we didn't know, we fixed up a pretty story. We fixed up a pretty story, and we convinced ourselves of it and we lived by it. And when I come along and show you it was no more than a pretty story, dreamed up because we had to have a story— *had* to have, I say—you are ready to read me out of chapel and to exile me. You'll have to do better than that, Herb. Much better than that."

He patted the gun. "I can do better than that," he said.

"Jon, you are mad."

"And you are a fool," said Jon.

At first he had been afraid, then he had been angry, and now there was only contempt—only contempt for them, huddled in the corridor, voicing feeble threats.

"What did you do with Joshua?" he asked.

46

"We tied him up," said Herb.

"Go back and untie him and send me up some food," he said.

They wavered. He made a threatening motion with the gun. "Go," he said.

They ran.

He slammed the door and went back to the telescope.

He found six planets, and two had atmospheres, No. 2 and No. 5. He looked at his watch, and many hours had gone by. Joshua had still not appeared. There had been no rap at the door. There was no food and water. He climbed the steps to the navigator's chair again.

The star was far astern. The velocity had slid way off but was still too fast.

He pulled the lever back and watched the velocity indicator drop. It was safe to do that—he hoped it was safe to do it. The Ship was thirty million out and it should be safe to cut velocity.

He studied the board and it was clearer now, more understandable—there were more things he knew about. It was not so hard, he thought. It would not be too hard. You had time. You had plenty of time. You had to plan ahead, but you had time to do it.

He studied the board and he found the computator he had missed before, the little metal brain—and that was how you told the Ship. That was what he had missed before—that was what he had wondered about—how to tell the Ship. And this was the way you told it. You told the little brain.

The one word—*automatic*—kept on hounding him. He found the stud that was labeled *telescope* and the one that was labeled *orbit* and still another that was labeled *landing*.

That was it, he thought. After all the worry, after all the fears, it was as simple as all that. For that would have been the way those back on Earth would have made the Ship. Simple. Simple beyond belief. So simple that any fool could land it. Just anyone at all who could punch a button. For certainly they must have feared or guessed what might happen on the Ship after several generations. They must have known how Earth would be forgotten and that there would be a cultural adaptation to the Ship. Feared or guessed—or planned? Was the cul-

47

ture of the Ship a part of the master plan? Could the Folk have lived through a thousand years if they had known of the purpose and the destination?

And the answer seemed to be that they wouldn't have been able to, for they would have felt robbed and cheated, would have gone mad with the knowledge that they were no more than carriers of life, that their lives and the lives of many generations after them would be canceled out so that after many generations their descendants could arrive at the target planet.

There had been only one way to beat that situation—and that was to forget what it was all about. And that is what had happened, and it had been for the best.

The Folk, after the first few generations, had lived their little lives in the little circle of their home-grown culture, and that had been enough. After that the thousand years had been as nothing, for no one knew about the thousand years.

And all the time the Ship bored on through space, heading for the target, heading straight and true.

Jon Hoff went down to the telescope and centered Planet V and clamped over the radar controls that would hold it centered. He went back to the computator and pushed the stud that said *telescope* and the other stud that said *orbit*.

Then he sat down to wait. There was nothing more to do.

Planet V was death.

The analyzer told the story. The atmosphere was mostly methane, the gravity thirty times too great, the pressure beneath the boiling clouds of methane close to a thousand atmospheres. There were other factors, too. But any one of those three would have been enough.

Jon Hoff pulled the Ship out of its orbit, headed it sunward. Back at the telescope, he found Planet II, locked it in the sights, tied in the computator and sat down to wait again.

One chance more and that was all they had. For all of the planets, only two had atmospheres. It had to be Planet II or none.

And if the second planet turned out to be death as well, what then?

There was one answer. There could be no other. Head the Ship toward another star, build up velocity and hope —hope that in another several generations the Folk could find a planet they could live on.

He was hungry—his belly gaunt and sore. He had found a water cooler with a few cups of liquid still intact, but he'd drunk the last of that two days before.

Joshua had not come back. There had been no sign from the Folk. Twice he had opened the door and gone out into the corridor, ready to make a dash for food and water, then had reconsidered and gone back in again. For he couldn't take the chance. He couldn't take the chance that they would sight him and run him down and not let him go back to the control room.

But the time would come before too long when he'd have to take a chance—when he'd have to make the dash. For before another day was gone he might be too weak to make it. And there were many days ahead before they would reach Planet II.

The time would come when he'd have no choice. That he could stick it out was impossible. If he did not get food and water, he'd be a useless, crawling hulk with the strength and mind gone out of him by the time they reached the planet.

He went back to the control board and looked things over. It seemed to be all right. The Ship was still building up velocity. The monitor on the computator was clocking its blue light and chuckling to itself, saying, *Everything's all right, everything's all right.*

Then he went back down the steps and to the corner where he'd been sleeping. He lay down and curled himself into a ball, trying to squeeze his belly together so that it wouldn't nag him. He shut his eyes and tried to go to sleep.

With his ear against the metal he could hear the pulsing of the engines far back in their room—the song of power that ran through all the Ship. And he remembered how he had thought a man might have to live with a ship to run her. But it hadn't turned out that way, although he could see how a man might learn to live with a ship, how a ship might become a part of him.

He dozed off and woke, then dozed off again—and

this time there was a voice shouting and someone hammering at the door.

He came to his feet in one lithe motion, scrambled for the door, the key already in his fist, stabbing at the lock. He jerked the door open and Mary stumbled in. She carried a great square can in one hand a huge sack in the other, and boiling down the corridor toward the door was a running mob that brandished clubs and screamed.

Jon reached down and hauled Mary clear, then slammed the door and locked it. He heard the running bodies thud against the door and then the clubs pounding at it and the people screaming.

Jon stooped above his wife. "Mary," he said, his voice choking and his throat constricting. "Mary."

"I had to come," she said, and she was crying when she said it. "I had to come, no matter what you did."

"What I have done," he said, "has been for the best. It was a part of the Plan, Mary. I am convinced of that. Part of the Master Plan. The people back on Earth had it all planned out. I just happened to be the one who—"

"You are a heretic," she said. "You've destroyed our Belief. You have set the Folk at one another's throat. You . . ."

"I know the truth," he said. "I know the purpose of the Ship."

She reached up her hands and cupped his face between her palms and pulled his head down and cuddled him.

"I don't care," she said. "I don't care. Not any more, I don't. I did at first. I was angry with you, Jon. I was ashamed of you. I almost died of shame. But when they killed Joshua . . ."

"What was that?"

"They killed Joshua. They beat him to death. And he's not the only one. There were others who wanted to come and help you. Just a few of them. They killed them, too. There's killing in the Ship. And hate. And suspicion. And all sorts of ugly rumors. It never was like that before. Not before you took away Belief."

A culture shattered, he thought. Shattered in the matter of an hour. A belief twitched away in the breadth of one split second. There was madness and killing. Of course there'd be.

"They are afraid," he said. "Their security is gone."

"I tried to come earlier," Mary said. "I knew you must be hungry and I was afraid there'd be no water. But I had to wait until no one was watching."

He held her tight against him and his eyes were a little dim.

"There's food," she said, "and water. I brought all that I could carry."

"My wife," he said. "My darling wife . . ."

"There's food, Jon. Why don't you eat?"

He rose and pulled her to her feet.

"In just a minute," he said, "I'll eat in just a minute. First I want to show you something. I want to show you Truth."

He led her up the steps.

"Look out there," he said. "That is where we're going. This is where we've been. No matter what we might have told ourselves, that out there is Truth."

Planet II was the Holy Pictures come to life entire. There were Trees and Brooks, Flowers and Grass, Sky and Clouds, Wind and Sunshine.

Mary and Jon stood beside the navigator's chair and stared out through the vision plate.

The analyzer gurgled slightly and spat out its report. *Safe for humans,* said the printed slip, adding a great deal of data about atmospheric composition, bacterial count, violet-ray intensity and many other things. But the one conclusion was enough. *Safe for humans.*

Jon reached out his hand for the master switch in the center of the Board. "This is it," he said. "This is the end of the thousand years."

He turned the switch and the dials all clicked to zero. The needles found dead center. The song of power died out in the Ship and there was the olden silence—the silence of long ago, of the time when the stars were streaks and the walls were floors.

Then they heard the sound—the sound of human wailing, as an animal might howl.

"They are afraid," said Mary. "They are scared to death. They won't leave the Ship."

And she was right, he knew. That was something that he had not thought of—that they would not leave the Ship.

They had been tied to it for many generations. They had looked to it for shelter and security. To them the vastness of the world outside, the never-ending Sky, the lack of a boundary of any sort at all, would be sodden terror.

Somehow or other they would have to be driven from the Ship—literally driven from it, and the Ship locked tight so they could not fight their way back in again. For the Ship was ignorance and cowering; it was a shell outgrown; it was the womb from which the race would be born anew.

Mary asked, "What will they do to us? I never thought of that. We can't hide from them, or . . ."

"Not anything," said Jon. "They won't do anything. Not while I have this." He slapped the gun at his side.

"But, Jon, this killing . . ."

"There won't be any killing. They will be afraid, and the fear will force them to do what must be done. After a time, maybe a long time, they will come to their senses, and then there will be no further fear. But to start with there is a need of . . ." The knowledge stirred within his brain, the knowledge implanted there by the strange machine. "Leadership," he said. "That is what they'll need —someone to lead them, to tell them what to do, to help them to work together."

He thought bitterly, I believed that it had ended, but it hasn't ended. Bringing down the Ship was not enough. I must go on from there. No matter what I do, as long as I live, there will be no end to it.

There was the getting settled and the learning once again. There were the books in the chest, he remembered, more than half the chest packed full of books. Basic text, perhaps. The books that would be needed for the starting over.

And somewhere, too, instructions? Instructions left with the books for a man like him to read and carry out? INSTRUCTIONS TO BE PUT INTO EFFECT AFTER LANDING: That would be the notation the envelope would carry, or another very like it, and he'd tear the envelope open and there would be folded pages.

Once before, in another letter, there had been folded pages.

And the second letter? There would be one, he was sure.

"It was planned on Earth," he said. "Every step was planned. They planned the great forgetting as the only way that humans could carry out the flight. They planned the heresy that handed down the knowledge. They made the Ship so simple that anyone could handle it—anyone at all. They looked ahead and saw what was bound to happen. Their planning has been just a jump ahead of us every moment."

He stared out the vision plate at the sweep of land, at the Trees and Grass and Sky. "I wouldn't be surprised," he said, "if they figured out how to drive us off the Ship."

A loud-speaker came to life and talked throughout the Ship, so that everyone might hear. *Now hear this,* it said, the old recording just a little scratchy. *Now hear this. You must leave the Ship within the next twelve hours. At the expiration of that time a deadly gas will be released inside the Ship.*

Jon reached out his hand to Mary. "I was right," he said. "They planned it to the last. They're still that jump ahead of us."

They stood there, the two of them, thinking of those people who had planned so well, who had thought so far ahead, who had known the problems and had planned against them.

"Come on," he said. "Let's go."

"Jon."

"Yes?"

"Can we have children now?"

"Yes," he said. "We can have children. Anyone who wishes may. On the Ship there were so many of us. Now on this planet there are so few of us."

"There is room," said Mary. "Room to spare."

He unlocked the control room door, carefully locked it behind him. They went down the darkened corridors.

The loud-speaker took up again: *Now hear this. Now hear this. You must leave the Ship . . .*

Mary shrank against him and he felt the trembling of her body.

"Jon. Are we going out now? Are we going out?"

53

Frightened. Of course she was frightened. He was frightened, too. One does not slough off entirely the fears of generations even in the light of truth.

"Not right away," he said. "I've got to look for something."

But the time would come when they would have to leave the Ship, step out into the frightening vastness of the planet—naked and afraid and shorn of the security of the enclosing shell that could be theirs no longer.

But when that time came, he would know what to do. He was sure he would.

For when the men of Earth had planned so well, they would not have failed in the final moment to have left a letter of instructions for the starting over.

MIRAGE

THEY came out of the Martian night, six pitiful little creatures looking for a seventh.

They stopped at the edge of the campfire's lighted circle and stood there, staring with their owlish eyes at the three Earthmen.

The Earthmen froze at whatever they were doing.

"Quiet," said Wampus Smith, talking out of the corner of his bearded lips. "They'll come in if we don't make a move."

From far away came a faint, low moaning, floating in across the wilderness of sand and jagged pinnacles of rock and the great stone buttes.

The six stood just at the firelight's edge. The reflection of the flames touched their fur with highlights of red and blue and their bodies seemed to shimmer against the backdrop of the darkness on the desert.

"Venerables," Nelson said to Richard Webb across the fire.

Webb's breath caught in his throat. Here was a thing he had never hoped to see. A thing that no human being could ever hope to see—six of the Venerables of Mars walking in out of the desert and the darkness, standing in the firelight. There were many men, he knew, who would claim that the race was now extinct, hunted down, trapped out, hounded to extinction by the greed of the human sand men.

The six had seemed the same at first, six beings without a difference; but now, as Webb looked at them, he saw those minor points of bodily variation which marked each one of them as a separate individual. Six of them, Webb thought, and there should be seven.

Slowly they came forward, walking deeper into the campfire's circle. One by one they sat down on the sand facing the three men. No one said a word and the tension built up in the circle of the fire, while far toward the north the thing kept up its keening, like a sharp, thin knife blade cutting through the night.

"Human glad," Wampus Smith said, finally, talking in the patois of the desert. "He waited long."

One of the creatures spoke, its words half English, half Martian, all of it pure gibberish to the ear that did not know.

"We die," it said. "Human hurt for long. Human help some now. Now we die, human help?"

"Human sad," said Wampus and even while he tried to make his voice sad, there was elation in it, a trembling eagerness, a quivering as a hound will quiver when the scent is hot.

"We are six," the creature said. "Six not enough. We need another one. We do not find the Seven, we die. Race die forever now."

"Not forever," Smith told them.

The Venerable insisted. "Forever. There other Sixes. No other Seven."

"How can human help?"

"Human know. Human have Seven somewhere?"

Wampus shook his head. "Where we have Seven?"

"In cage. On Earth. For human to see."

Wampus shook his head again. "No Seven on Earth."

"There was one," Webb said softly. "In a zoo."

"Zoo," said the creature, tonguing the unfamiliar word. "We mean that. In cage."

"It died," said Webb. "Many years ago."

"Human have one," the creature insisted. "Here on planet. Hid out. To trade."

55

"No understand," said Wampus but Webb knew from the way he said it that he understood.

"Find Seven. Do not kill it. Hide it. Knowing we come. Knowing we pay."

"Pay? What pay?"

"City," said the creature. "Old city."

"That's your city," Nelson said to Webb. "The ruins you are hunting."

"Too bad we haven't got a Seven," Wampus said. "We could hand it over and they'd lead us to the ruins."

"Human hurt for long," the creature said. "Human kill all Sevens. Have good fur. Women human wear it. High pay for Seven fur."

"Lord, yes," said Nelson. "Fifty thousand for one at the trading post. A cool half million for a four-skin cape made up in New York."

Webb sickened at the thought of it, at the casual way in which Nelson mentioned it. It was illegal now, of course, but the law had come too late to save the Venerables. Although a law, come to think of it, should not have been necessary. A human being, in all rightness—an intelligent form of life, in all rightness, should not hunt down and kill another intelligent being to strip off its pelt and sell it for fifty thousand dollars.

"No Seven hid," Wampus was saying. "Law says friends. No dare hurt Seven. No dare hide Seven."

"Law far off," said the creature. "Human his own law."

"Not us," said Wampus. "We don't monkey with the law."

And that's a laugh, thought Webb.

"You help?" asked the creature.

"Try, maybe," Wampus told them cagily. "No good, though. You can't find. Human can't find."

"You find. We show city."

"We watch," said Wampus. "Close watch. See Seven, bring it. Where you be?"

"Canyon mouth."

"Good," said Wampus. "Deal?"

"Deal," said the creature.

Slowly the six of them got to their feet and turned back to the night again. At the edge of the firelit circle they stopped. The spokesman turned back to the three men.

"By," he said.

"Goodbye," said Wampus.

Then they were gone, back into the desert.

The three men sat and listened for a long time, not knowing what they listened for, but with ears taut to hear the slightest sound, trying to read out of sound some of the movement of life that surged all around the fire.

On Mars, thought Webb, one always listens. That is the survival price. To watch and listen and be still and quiet. And ruthless, too. To strike before another thing can strike. To see or hear a danger and be ready for it, to be half a second quicker than it is quick. And to recognize that danger once you see or hear it.

Finally Nelson took up again the thing he had been doing when the six arrived, whetting his belt knife to a razor sharpness on a pocket whetstone.

The soft, sleek whirr of metal traveling over stone sounded like a heartbeat, a pulse that did not originate within the firelight circle, but something that came out of the darkness, the pulse and beat of the wilderness itself.

Wampus said: "It's too bad, Lars, that we don't know where to pick us up a Seven."

"Yeah," said Lars.

"Might turn a good deal," Wampus said. "Likely to be treasure in that old city. All the stories say so."

Nelson grunted. "Just stories."

"Stones," said Wampus. "Stones so bright and polished they could put your eyes out. Sacks of them. Tire a man out just packing them away."

"Wouldn't need more than one load," Nelson declared. "Just one load would set you up for life."

Webb saw that both of them were looking at him, squinting their eyes against the firelight.

He said, almost angrily, "I don't know about the treasure."

"You heard the stories," Wampus said.

Webb nodded. "Let's say it this way. I'm not interested in the treasure. I don't expect to find any."

"Wouldn't mind if you did, would you?" Lars asked.

"It doesn't matter," Webb told them. "One way or the other."

"What do you know about this city?" Wampus de-

57

manded, and it wasn't just conversation, it was a question asked with an answer expected, for a special purpose. "You been muttering around and dropping hints here and there but you never came cold out and told us."

For a moment, Webb stared at the man. Then he spoke slowly. "Just this. I figured out where it might be. From a knowledge of geography and geology and some understanding of the rise of cultures. I figured where the grass and wood and water would have been when Mars was new and young. I tried to locate, theoretically, the likeliest place for a civilization to arise. That's all there's to it."

"And you never thought of treasure?"

"I thought of finding out something about the Martian culture," Webb said. "How it rose and why it fell and what it might be like."

Wampus spat. "You aren't even sure there is a city," he said disgustedly.

"Not until just now," said Webb. "Now I know there is."

"From what them little critters said?"

Webb nodded. "From what they said. That's right."

Wampus grunted and was silent.

Webb watched the two across the campfire from him.

They think I'm soft, he thought. They despise me because I'm soft. They would leave me in a minute if it served their purpose or they'd put a knife into me without a second thought if that should serve their purpose, if there was something I had that they wanted.

There had been no choice, he realized. He could not have gone alone into this wilderness, for if he'd tried he probably wouldn't have lived beyond the second day. It took special knowledge to live here and a special technique and a certain kind of mind. A man had to develop a high survival factor to walk into Mars beyond the settlements.

And the settlements were now very far away. Somewhere to the east.

"Tomorrow," Wampus said, "we change directions. We go north instead of west."

Webb said nothing. His hand slid around cautiously and touched the gun at his belt, to make sure that it was there.

It had been a mistake to hire these two, he knew. But probably none of the others would have been better. They were all of a breed, a toughened, vicious band of men who roamed the wilderness, hunting, trapping, mining, taking what they found. Wampus and Nelson had been the only two at the post when he had arrived. All the other sand men had gone a week before, back to their hunting grounds.

At first they had been respectful, almost fawning. But as the days went on they felt surer of their ground and had grown insolent. Now Webb knew that he'd been taken for a sucker. The two stayed at the post, he knew now, for no other reason than that they were without a grubstake. He was that grubstake. He supplied them with the trappings they needed to get back into the wilderness. Once he had been a grubstake, now he was a burden.

"I said," declared Wampus, "that tomorrow we go north."

Webb still said nothing.

"You heard me, didn't you?" asked Wampus.

"The first time," Webb said.

"We go north," said Wampus, "and we travel fast."

"You got a Seven staked out somewhere?"

Lars snickered. "Ain't that the damnedest thing you ever heard of? Takes seven of them. Now with us, it just takes a man and woman."

"I asked you," said Webb to Wampus, "if you have a Seven caged up somewhere?"

"No," said Wampus. "We just go north, that's all."

"I hired you to take me west."

Wampus snarled at him. "I thought you'd say that, Webb. I just wanted to know exactly how you felt about it."

"You want to leave me stranded here," said Webb. "You took my money and agreed to guide me. Now you have something else to do. You either have a Seven or you think you know where you can find one. And if I knew and talked, you would be in danger. So there's only one of two things that you can do with me. You can kill me or you can leave me and let something else do the job for you."

Lars said: "We're giving you a choice, ain't we?"

59

Webb looked at Wampus and the man nodded. "You got your choice, Webb."

He could go for his gun, of course. He could get one of them, most likely, before the other one got him. But there would be nothing gained. He would be just as dead as if they shot him out of hand. As far as that went he was as good as dead anyhow, for hundreds of miles stretched between him and the settlements, and even if he were able to cross those many miles there was no guarantee that he could find the settlements.

"We're moving out right now," said Wampus. "Ain't smart to travel in the dark, but ain't the first time that we had to do it. We'll be up north in a day or two."

Lars nodded. "Once we get back to the settlements, Webb, we'll h'ist a drink to you."

Wampus joined in the spirit of the moment. "Good likker, Webb. We can afford good likker then."

Webb said nothing, did not move. He sat on the ground, relaxed.

And that, he told himself, was the thing that scared him. That he could sit and know what was about to happen and be so unconcerned about it.

Perhaps it had been the miles of wilderness that made it possible, the harsh, raw land and the vicious life that moved across the land—the ever-hungering, ever-hunting life that prowled and stalked and killed. Here life was stripped to its essentials and one learned that the line between life and death was a thin line at best.

"Well," said Wampus finally, "what will it be, Webb?"

"I think," said Webb gravely, "I think I'll take my chance on living."

Lars clucked his tongue against his teeth. "Too bad," he said. "We was hoping it'd be the other way around. Then we could take all the stuff. As it is, we got to leave you some."

"You can always sneak back," said Webb, "and shoot me as I sit here. It would be an easy thing."

"That," said Wampus, is not a bad idea."

Lars said: "Give me your gun, Webb. I'll throw it back to you when we leave. But we ain't taking a chance of you plugging us while we're getting ready."

Webb lifted his gun out of his holster and handed it

over. Still sitting where he was, he watched them pack and stow the supplies into the wilderness wagon.

Finally it was done.

"We're leaving you plenty to last," Wampus told him. "More than enough."

"Probably," said Webb. "You figure I can't last very long."

"If it was me," said Wampus, "I'd take it quick and easy."

Webb sat for a long time, listening to the motor of the wagon until it was out of hearing, then waiting for the gun blast that would send him toppling face forward into the flaming campfire.

But finally he knew that it would not come. He piled more fuel on the fire and crawled into his sleeping bag.

In the morning he headed east, following backward along the tracks of the wilderness wagon. They'd guide him, he knew, for a week or so, but finally they would disappear, brushed out by drifting sand and by the action of the weak and whining wind that sometimes blew across the bleakness of the wilderness.

At least while he followed them he would know he was going in the right direction. Although more than likely he would be dead before they faded out, for the wilderness crawled with too much sudden death for him to be sure of living from one moment to the next.

He walked with the gun hanging in his hand, watching every side, stopping at the top of the ridges to study the terrain in front of him before he moved down into it.

The unaccustomed pack which he had fashioned inexpertly out of his sleeping bag grew heavier as the day progressed and chafed his shoulders raw. The sun was warm, as warm as the night would be cold, and thirst mounted in his throat to choke him. Carefully he doled out sips of water from the scanty supply the two had left him.

He knew he would not get back. Somewhere between where he stood and the settlements he would die of lack of water, or of an insect bite, or beneath the jaws and fangs of some charging beast or from sheer exhaustion.

There was, once you thought it out, no reason why a man should try to get back, since there was utterly no chance that he would get back. But Webb didn't stop to reason it out; he set his face toward the east and followed the wagon tracks.

For there was a *humanness* in him that said he must try at least—that he must go as far as he could go, that he must avoid death as long as he could. So on he went, going as far as he could go and avoiding death.

He spotted the ant colony in time to circle it, but he circled it too closely and the insects, catching scent of food within their grasp, streamed out after him. It took a mile of running before he outdistanced them.

He saw the crouching beast camouflaged against the sand, where it was waiting for him, and shot it where it lay. Later in the day, when another monstrosity came tearing out from behind a rock outcropping, his bullet caught it between the eyes before it had covered half the distance.

For an hour he squatted, unmoving, on the sand, while a huge insect that looked like a bumblebee, but wasn't, hunted for the thing that it had sighted only a moment before. But since it could recognize a thing through motion only, it finally gave up and went away. Webb remained squatting for another half hour against the chance that it had not gone away but lurked somewhere watching for the motion it had sighted, to take up the hunt again.

These times he avoided death, but he knew that the hour would come when he would not see a danger, or, having seen it, would not move fast enough to stop it.

The mirages came to haunt him, to steal his eyes from the things that he should be watching. Mirages that flickered in the sky, with their feet upon the ground. Tantalizing pictures of things that could not be on Mars, of places that might have been there at one time—but that very long ago.

Mirages of broad, slow rivers with the slant of sail upon them. Mirages of green forests that stretched across the hills, so clear, so close, that one could see the little clumps of wild flowers that grew among the trees. And in some of them the hint of snow-capped mountains, in a world that knew no mountains.

He kept a watch for fuel as he went along, hoping to find a cache of "embalmed" wood cropping out of the sand—wood left over from that dim age when these hills and valleys had been forest-covered, wood that had escaped the ravages of time and now lay like the dried mummies of trees in the aridness of the desert.

But there was none to be found and he knew that more than likely he would have to spend a fireless night. He could not spend a night in the open without fire. If he tried it, he would be gobbled up an hour after twilight had set in.

He must somehow find shelter in one of the many caves of the weird rock formations that sprang out of the desert. Find a cave and clean out whatever might be in it, block its entrance with stones and boulders and sleep with gun in hand.

It had sounded easy when he thought of it, but while there were many caves, he was forced to reject them one by one since each of them had too large an opening to be closed against attack. A cave, he knew, with an un-closed mouth, would be no better than a trap.

The sun was less than an hour high when he finally spotted a cave that would serve the purpose, located on a ledge of stone jutting out of a steep hill.

From the bottom he stood long minutes surveying the hill. Nothing moved. There were no telltale flecks of color.

Slowly he started up, digging his feet into the shifting talus of the slope, fighting his way up foot by foot, stopping for long minutes to regain his breath and to survey the slope ahead.

Gaining the ledge, he moved cautiously toward the cave, gun leveled, for there was no telling what might come out of it.

He debated on his next move. Flash his light inside to see what was there? Or simply thrust his gun into the opening and spray the inside with its lethal charge?

There could be no squeamishness, he told himself. Better to kill a harmless thing than to run the chance of passing up a danger.

He heard no sound until the claws of the thing were scrabbling on the ledge behind him. He shot one quick glance over his shoulder and saw the beast almost on top of him, got the impression of gaping mouth and murder-ous fangs and tiny eyes that glinted with a stony cruelty.

There was no time to turn and fire. There was time for just one thing.

His legs moved like driving pistons, hurling his body at the cave. The stone lip caught his shoulder and ripped through his clothing, gashing his arm, but he was through, through and rolling free. Something brushed his face and he rolled over something that protested in a squeaking voice. Off in one corner there was a thing that mewed quietly to itself.

On his knees, Webb swung his gun around to face the opening of the cave, saw the great bulk of the beast that had charged him trying to squeeze its way inside.

It backed away and then a great paw came in, feeling this way and that, hunting for the food that crouched inside the cave.

Mouths jabbered at Webb, a dozen voices speaking in the lingo of the desert, and he heard them say:

"Human, human, kill, kill, kill."

Webb's gun spat and the paw went limp and was pulled slowly from the cave. The great gray body toppled and they heard it strike the slope below the ledge and go slithering away down the talus slope.

"Thanks, human," said the voices. "Thanks, human."

Slowly Webb sat down, cradling the gun in his lap.

All around him he heard the stir of life.

Sweat broke out on his forehead and he felt moisture running from his armpits down his sides.

What was in the cave? What was in here with him?

That they had talked to him didn't mean a thing. Half the so-called animals of Mars could talk the desert lingo —a vocabulary of a few hundred words, part of them Earthian, part of them Martian, part of them God-knew-what.

For here on Mars many of the animals were not animals at all, but simply degenerating forms of life that at one time must have formed a complex civilization. The Venerables, who still retained some of the shape of bipeds, would have reached the highest culture, but there must have been many varying degrees of culture, living by compromise or by tolerance.

"Safe," a voice told him. "Trust. Cave law."

"Cave law?"

"Kill in cave, no. Kill outside cave, yes. Safe in cave."

64

"I no kill," said Webb. "Cave law good."

"Human know cave law?"

Webb said: "Human keep cave law."

"Good," the voice told him. "All safe now."

Webb relaxed. He slipped his gun into his holster and took off his pack, laid it down alongside and rubbed his raw and blistered shoulders.

He could believe these things, he told himself. A thing so elemental and so simple as cave law was a thing that could be understood and trusted. It arose from a basic need, the need of the weaker life forms to forget their mutual differences and their mutual preying upon one another at the fall of night, the need to find a common sanctuary against the bigger and the more vicious creatures and the lonely killers who took over with the going of the sun.

A voice said, "Come light. Human kill."

Another voice said, "Human keep cave law in dark. No cave law in light. Human kill come light."

"Human no kill come light," said Webb.

"All human kill," said one of the things. "Human kill for fur. Human kill for food. We fur. We food."

"This human never kill," said Webb. "This human friend."

"Friend?" one of them asked. "We not know friend. Explain friend."

Webb didn't try. There was no use, he knew. They could not understand the word. It was foreign to this wilderness.

At last he asked, "Rocks here?"

One of the voices answered, "Rocks in cave. Human want rocks?"

"Pile in cave mouth," said Webb. "No killer get in."

They digested that for a while. Finally one of them spoke up. "Rock good."

They brought rocks and stones and, with Webb helping them, wedged the cave mouth tight.

It was too dark to see the things, but they brushed against him as they worked and some of them were soft and furry and others had hides like crocodiles that tore his skin as he brushed against them. And there was one that was soft and pulpy and gave him the creeps.

He settled down in one corner of the cave, with his

65

sleeping bag between his body and the wall. He would have liked to crawl into it, but that would have meant unpacking, and if he unpacked his supplies, he knew, there'd be none come morning.

Perhaps, he reasoned, the body heat of all the things in here would keep the cave from getting too cold. Cold yes, but not too cold for human life. It was, he knew, a gamble at best.

Sleep at night in friendship, kill one another and flee from one another with the coming of the dawn. Law, they called it. Cave law. Here was one for the books, here was something that was not even hinted at in all the archaeological tomes that he had ever read.

And he had read them all. There was something here on Mars that fascinated him. A mystery and a loneliness, an emptiness and a retrogression that haunted him and finally sent him out to try to pierce some of that mystery, to try to hunt for the reason for that retrogression, to essay to measure the greatness of the culture that in some far dim period had come tumbling down.

There had been some great work done along that line. Axelson with his scholarly investigation of the symbolic water jugs and Mason's sometimes fumbling attempt to trace the great migrations. Then there was Smith, who had traveled the barren world for years jotting down the wind-blown stories whispered by the little degenerating things about an ancient greatness and a golden past. Myths, most of them, of course, but some place, somewhere, lay the answer to the origin of the myths. Folklore does not leap full blown from the mind; it starts with a fact, and that fact is added to, and the two facts are distorted and you have a myth. But at the bottom, back of all of it, is the starting point of fact.

So it was, so it must be with the myth that told about the great and glowing city that had stood above all other things of Mars—a city that was known to the far ends of the planet.

A place of culture, Webb told himself, a place where all the achievements and all the dreams and every aspiration of the once-great planet would have come together.

And yet in more than a hundred years of hunting and of digging Earth's archaeologists had found no trace of any city, let alone that city of all cities. Kitchen middens and burial places and wretched huddling places where broken remnants of the great people had lived for a time—there were plenty of these. But no great city.

It must be somewhere, Webb was convinced. That myth could not lie, for it was told too often at too many different places by too many different animals that had once been people.

Mars fascinated me, he thought, and it still fascinates me, but now it will be the death of me, for there's death in its fascination. Death in the lonely stretches and death waiting on the buttes. Death in this cave, too, for they may kill me come the morning to prevent my killing them; they may keep their truce of the night just long enough to make an end of me.

The law of the cave? Some holdover from the ancient day, some memory of a now forgotten brotherhood? Or a device necessitated by the evil days that had come when the brotherhood had broken?

He laid his head back against the rock and closed his eyes and thought, if they kill me, they kill me, but I will not kill them. For there has been too much human killing on the planet Mars. I will repay part of the debt at least. I will not kill the ones who took me in.

He remembered himself creeping along the ledge outside the cave, debating whether he should have a look first or stick in the muzzle of his gun and sweep the cave as a simple way of being sure there would be nothing there to harm him.

I did not know, he said. I did not know.

A soft furry body brushed against him and a voice spoke to him. "Friend means no hurt? Friend means no kill?"

"No hurt," said Webb. "No kill."

"You saw six?" the voice asked.

Webb jerked from the wall and sat very still.

"You saw six?" the voice was insistent.

"I saw six," said Webb.

"When?"

"One sun."

"Where six?"

"Canyon mouth," said Webb. "Wait at canyon mouth."

"You hunt Seven?"

"No," said Webb. "I go home."

"Other humans?"

"They north," said Webb. "They hunt Seven north."

"They kill Seven?"

"Catch Seven," said Webb. "Take Seven to six. See city."

"Six promise?"

"Six promise," said Webb.

"You good human. You friend human. You no kill Seven."

"No kill," insisted Webb.

"All humans kill. Kill Seven sure. Seven good fur. Much pay. Many Sevens die for human."

"Law says no kill," declared Webb. "Human law says Seven friend. No kill friend."

"Law? Like cave law?"

"Like cave law," said Webb.

"You good friend of Seven?"

"Good friend of all," said Webb.

"I Seven," said the voice.

Webb sat quietly and let the numbness clear out of his brain.

"Seven," he finally said. "You go canyon mouth. Find six. They wait. Human friend glad."

"Human friend want city," said the creature. "Seven friend to human. Human find Seven. Human see city. Six promise."

Webb almost laughed aloud in bitterness. Here at last, the chance that he had hoped might come. Here at last, the thing that he had wanted, the thing he had come to Mars to do. And he couldn't do it. He simply couldn't do it.

"Human no go," he said. "Human die. No food. No water. Human die."

"We care for human," Seven told him. "No friend human before. All kill humans. Friend human come. We care for it."

Webb was silent for a while, thinking.

Then he asked: "You give human food? You find human water?"

"Take care," said Seven.

"How Seven know I saw six?"

"Human tell. Human think. Seven know."

So that was it—telepathy. Some vestige of a former

68

power, some attribute of a magnificent culture, not quite forgotten yet. How many of the other creatures in this cave would have it, too?

"Human go with Seven?" Seven asked.

"Human go," said Webb.

He might as well, he told himself. Going east, back toward the settlements, was no solution to his problem. He knew he'd never reach the settlements. His food would run out. His water would run out. Some beast would catch him and make a meal of him. He didn't have a chance.

Going with the little creature that stood beside him in the darkness of the cave, he might have a chance. Not too good a chance, perhaps, but at least a chance. There would be food and water, or at least a chance of food and water. There would be another to help him watch for the sudden death that roamed the wilderness, to warn him, to help him recognize the danger.

"Human cold," said Seven.

"Cold," admitted Webb.

"One cold," said Seven. "Two warm."

The furry thing crawled into his arms, put its arms around his body. After a moment, he put his arms around it.

"Sleep," said Seven. "Warm. Sleep."

Webb ate the last of his food, and the seven Venerables told him, "We care."

"Human die," Webb insisted. "No food. Human die."

"We take care," the seven little creatures told him, standing in a row. "Later we take care."

He took it to mean that there was no food for him now, but later there would be.

They took up the march again.

It was an interminable thing, that march. A thing to make a man cry out in his sleep. A thing to shiver over when they had been lucky enough to find wood and sat hunched around the fire. Day after endless day of sand and rock, of crawling up to a high ridge and plunging down the other side, of slogging through the heat across the level land that had been sea bottom in the days long gone.

It became a song, a drum beat, a three-note marching cadence that rang through the human's head, an endless thing that hammered in his brain through the day and stayed with him hours after they had stopped for night. Until he was dizzy with it, until his brain was drugged with the hammer of it, so that his eyes refused to focus and the gun bead was a fuzzy globe when he had to use the weapon against the crawling things and charging things and flying things that came at them out of nowhere.

Always there were the mirages, the everlasting mirages of Mars that seemed to lie just beneath the surface of reality. Flickering pictures painted in the sky the water and the trees and the long green sweep of grass that Mars had not known for countless centuries. As if, Webb told himself, the past were very close behind him, as if the past might still exist and were trying to catch up, reluctant to be left behind in the march of time.

He lost count of the days and steeled himself against the speculation of how much longer it might be, until it seemed that it would go on forever, that they would never stop, that they would face each morning the barren wilderness they must stagger through until the fall of night.

He drank the last of the water and reminded them he could not live without it.

"Later," they told him. "Water later."

That was the day they came to the city, and there, deep in a tunnel far beneath the topmost ruins there was water, water dripping, drop by slow and tantalizing drop, from a broken pipe. Dripping water, and that was a wondrous thing on Mars.

The seven drank sparingly, as they had been steeled for century upon century to get along with little water, had adapted themselves to this and it was no hardship for them. But Webb lay for hours beside the broken pipe, holding cupped hands to collect a little before he lapped it down, lying there in the coolness that was a blessed thing.

He slept and awoke and drank again, and he was rested and no longer thirsty, but his body cried for food. And there was no food nor anyone to get him food. For the little ones were gone.

They will come back, he said. They are gone for just a little while and will be back again. They have gone to get me food and they will bring it to me. And he thought very kindly of them.

He picked his way upward through the tunnel down which they'd come and at last came to the ruins that lay on the hill that thrust upward from the surrounding country so that when one stood on the hill's top there were miles of distance, dropping away on every side.

There wasn't much that one could see of the ruined city. It would have been entirely possible to walk past the hill and not know the city was there. During thousands of years it had crumbled and fallen in upon itself and some of it had dissolved to dust, and the sand had crept in and covered it and sifted among its fragments until it was simply a part of the hill.

Here and there Webb found broken fragments of chiseled masonry and here and there a shard of pottery, but a man could have walked past these, if he had not been looking, and taken them for no more than another rock scattered among the trillions of fragmentary rocks littered on the surface of the planet.

The tunnel, he found, led down into the bowels of the fallen city, into the burial mound of the fallen greatness and the vanished glory of a proud people whose descendants now scuttled animal-like in the ancient deserts and talked in an idiom that was no more than a memory of the literacy that must have flourished once in the city on the hill.

In the tunnel Webb found evidence of solid blocks of carven stone, broken columns, paving blocks and something that seemed at one time to have been a beautifully executed statue.

At the end of the tunnel he cupped his hands at the pipe and drank again, then went back to the surface and sat on the ground beside the tunnel mouth and stared out across the emptiness of Mars.

It would take power and tools and many men to uncover and sift the evidence of the city. It would take years of painstaking, scholarly work—and he didn't even have a shovel. And worst of all, he had no time. For if the seven did not show up with food he would one day go down into the darkness of the tunnel and there eventually join his human dust with the ancient dust of this alien world.

There had been a shovel, he remembered, and Wampus and Lars, when they deserted him, had left it for him. A rare consideration, surely, he told himself. But of the supplies which he had carried away from the campfire that long gone morning there were just two things left, his sleeping bag and the pistol at his belt. All else he could get along without, those two were things that he had to have.

An archaeologist, he thought. An archaeologist sitting on top of the greatest find that any archaeologist had ever made and not able to do a single thing about it.

Wampus and Lars had thought that there would be treasure here. And there was no certain treasure, no treasure revealed and waiting for the hands of men to take. He had thought of glory, and there was no glory. He had thought of knowledge, and without a shovel and some time, there simply was no knowledge. No knowledge beyond the bare knowing that he had been right, that the city did exist.

And yet there was certain other knowledge gained along the way. The knowledge that the seven types of the Venerables did in fact still exist, that from this existence the race might still continue despite the guns and snares and the greed and guile of Earthmen who had hunted Seven for its fifty-thousand-dollar pelt.

Seven little creatures, seven different sexes. All of them essential to the continuance of the race. Six little creatures looking for the seventh, and he had found the seventh. Because he had found the seventh, because he had been the messenger, there would be at least one new generation of the Venerables to carry on the race.

What use, he thought, to carry on a race that had failed its purpose?

He shook his head.

You can't play God, he said. You can't presume to judge. Either there is a purpose in all things or there's no purpose in anything, and who is there to know?

Either there is purpose that I reached this city or there is no purpose. There is a purpose that I may die here or it is possible that my dying here will be no more than another random factor in the great machination of pure chance that moves the planets through their courses and brings a man homeward at the end of day.

And there was another knowledge—the knowledge of the endless reaches and the savage loneliness that was the Martian wilderness. The knowledge of that and the queer, almost nonhuman detachment that it fused into the human soul.

Lessons, he thought.

The lesson that one man is an insignificant flyspeck crawling across the face of eternity. The lesson that one life is a relatively unimportant thing when it stands face to face with the overriding reality of the miracle of all creation.

He got up and stood at his full height and knew his insignificance and his humility in the empty sweep of land that fell away on every side and in the arching sky that vaulted overhead from horizon to horizon and in the utter silence that lay upon the land and sky.

Starving was a lonely and an awful business.

Some deaths are swift and clean. But starving is not one of these.

The seven did not come. Webb waited for them, and because he still felt kindly toward them he found excuses for them. They did not realize, he told himself, how short a time a man may go without nourishment. The strange mating, he told himself, involving seven personalities, probably was a complicated procedure and might take a great deal more time than one usually associated with such phenomena. Or something might have happened to them, they might be having trouble of their own. As soon as they had worked it out they would come, and they would bring him food.

So he starved with kindly thoughts and with a great deal more patience than a man in dissimilar circumstances might be expected to do.

And he found, even when he felt the lassitude of undernourishment creeping along his muscles and his bones, even when the sharp pangs of hunger had settled to a gnawing horror that never left him, even when he slept, that his mind was not affected by the ravages that his body was undergoing; that his brain, apparently, was sharpened by the lack of food, that it seemed to step aside from his tortured body and become a separate entity that drew in upon itself and knotted all its faculties

73

into a hard-bound bundle that was scarcely aware of external factors.

He sat for long hours upon a polished rock, perhaps part of that once-proud city, which he found just a few yards from the tunnel mouth, and stared out across the sun-washed wilderness that stretched for miles toward a horizon that it never seemed to reach. He sought for purpose with a sharp-edged mind that probed at the roots of existence and of happenstance and sought to evolve out of the random factors that moved beneath the surface of the universe's orderliness some evidence of a pattern that would be understandable to the human mind. Often he thought he had it, but it always slid away from him like quicksilver escaping from a clutching hand.

If Man was ever to find the answer, he knew, it must be in a place like this, where there was no distraction, where there was a distance and a barrenness that built up to a vast impersonality which emphasized and underscored the inconsequence of the thinker. For if the thinker introduced himself as a factor out of proportion to the fact, then the whole problem was distorted and the equation, if equation there be, could never be solved.

At first he had tried to hunt animals for food, but strangely, while the rest of the wilderness swarmed with vicious life that hunted timid life, the area around the city was virtually deserted, as if some one had drawn a sacred chalk mark around it. On his second day of hunting he killed a small thing that on Earth could have been a mouse. He built a fire and cooked it and later hunted up the sundried skin and sucked and chewed at it for the small nourishment that it might contain. But after that he did not kill a thing, for there was nothing to be killed.

Finally he came to know the seven would not come, that they never had intended to come, that they had deserted him exactly as his two human companions had deserted him before. He had been made a fool, he knew, not once, but twice.

He should have kept on going east after he had started. He should not have come back with Seven to find the other six who waited at the canyon's mouth.

You might have made it to the settlements, he told himself. You just might have made it. Just possibly have made it.

74

East. East toward the settlements.

Human history is a trying—a trying for the impossible —and attaining it. There is no logic, for if humanity had waited upon logic it would still be a cave-living and an earth-bound race.

Try, said Webb, not knowing exactly what he said.

He walked down the hill again and started out across the wilderness, heading toward the east. For there was no hope upon the hill and there was hope toward the east.

A mile from the base of the hill, he fell. He staggered, falling and rising, for another mile. He crawled a hundred yards. It was there the seven found him.

"Food!" he cried at them and he had a feeling that although he cried it in his mind there was no sound in his mouth. "Food! Water!"

"We take care," they said, and lifted him, holding him in a sitting position.

"Life," Seven told him, "is in many husks. Like nested boxes that fit inside each other. You live one and you peel it off and there's another life."

"Wrong," said Webb. "You do not talk like that. Your thought does not flow like that. There is something wrong."

"There is an inner man," said Seven. "There are many inner men."

"The subconscious," said Webb and while he said it in his mind, he knew that no word, no sound came out of his mouth. And he knew now, too, that no words were coming out of Seven's mouth, that here were words that could not be expressed in the patois of the desert, that here were thoughts and knowledge that could not belong to a thing that scuttled, fearsome, through the Martian wilderness.

"You peel an old life off and you step forth in a new and shining life," said Seven, "but you must know the way. There is a certain technique and a certain preparation. If there is no preparation and no technique, the job is often bungled."

"Preparation," said Webb. "I have no preparation. I do not know about this."

"You are prepared," said Seven. "You were not before, but now you are."

"I thought," said Webb.

"You thought," said Seven, "and you found a partial answer. Well-fed, earth-bound, arrogant, there would have been no answer. You found humility."

"I do not know the technique," said Webb. "I do not . . ."

"We know the technique," Seven said. "We take care."

The hilltop where the dead city lay shimmered, and there was a mirage on it. Out of the dead mound of its dust rose the pinnacles and spires, the buttresses and the flying bridges of a city that shone with color and with light; out of the sand came the blaze of garden beds of flowers and the tall avenues of trees and a music that came from the slender bell towers.

There was grass beneath his feet instead of sand blazing with the heat of the Martian noon. There was a path that led up the terraces of the hill toward the wonder city that reared upon its heights. There was the distant sound of laughter and there were flecks of color moving on the distant streets and along the walls and through the garden paths.

Webb swung around and the seven were not there. Nor was the wilderness. The land stretched away on every hand and it was not wilderness, but a breath-taking place with groves of trees and roads and flowing water courses.

He turned back to the city again and watched the movement of the flecks of color.

"People," he said.

And Seven's voice, coming to him from somewhere, from elsewhere, said: "People from the many planets. And from beyond the planets. And some of your own people you will find among them. For you are not the first."

Filled with wonder, a wonder that was fading, that would be entirely faded before he reached the city, Webb started walking up the path.

Wampus Smith and Lars Nelson came to the hill many days late. They came on foot because the wilderness wagon had broken down. They came without food except the little food they could kill along the way; and they came with no more than a few drops of water slosh-

76

ing in their canteens—and there was no water to be found.

There, a short distance from the foot of the hill, they found the sun-dried mummy of a man face downward on the sand, and when they turned him over they saw who he was.

Wampus stared across the body at Lars. "How did he get here?" he croaked.

"I don't know," said Lars. "He never could have made it, not knowing the country and on foot. And he wouldn't have traveled this way anyhow. He would have headed east, back to the settlements."

They pawed through his clothing and found nothing. But they took his gun, for the charges in their own were running very low.

"What's the use?" said Lars. "We can't make it, Wampus."

"We can try," said Wampus.

Above the hill a mirage flickered—a city with shining turrets and dizzy pinnacles and rows of trees and fountains that flashed with leaping water. To their ears came, or seemed to come, the sound of many bells.

Wampus spat with lips that were cracked and dried, spat with no saliva in his mouth.

"Them damn mirages," he said. "They drive a man half crazy."

"They seem so close," said Lars. "So close and real. As if they were someplace else and were trying to break through."

Wampus spat again. "Let's get going," he said.

The two men turned toward the east and, as they moved, they left staggering, uneven tracks through the sand of Mars.

BEACHHEAD

THERE was nothing, absolutely nothing, that could stop a human planetary survey party. It was a specialized unit created for and charged with one purpose only—

to establish a bridgehead on an alien planet, to blast out the perimeters of that bridgehead and establish a base where there would be some elbow room. Then hold that elbow room against all comers until it was time to go.

After the base was once established, the brains of the party got to work. They turned the place inside out. They put it on tape and captured it within the chains of symbols they scribbled in their field books. They pictured it and wrote it and plotted it and reduced it to a neat assembly of keyed and symbolic facts to be inserted in the galactic files.

If there was life, and sometimes there was, they prodded it to get reaction. Sometimes the reaction was extremely violent, and other times it was much more dangerously subtle. But there were ways in which to handle both the violent and the subtle, for the legionnaires and their robots were trained to a razor's edge and knew nearly all the answers.

There was nothing in the galaxy so far known that could stop a human survey party.

Tom Decker sat at ease in the empty lounge and swirled the ice in the highball glass, well contented, watching the first of the robots emerge from the bowels of the cargo space. They dragged a conveyor belt behind them as they emerged, and Decker, sitting idly, watched them drive supports into the ground and rig up the belt.

A door clicked open back of Decker and he turned his head.

"May I come in, sir?" Doug Jackson asked.

"Certainly," said Decker.

Jackson walked to the great curving window and looked out. "What does it look like, sir?" he asked.

Decker shrugged. "Another job," he said. "Six weeks. Six months. Depends on what we find."

Jackson sat down beside him. "This one looks tough," he said. "Jungle worlds always are a bit meaner than any of the others."

Decker grunted at him. "A job. That's all. Another job to do. Another report to file. Then they'll either send out an exploitation gang or a pitiful bunch of bleating colonists."

"Or," said Jackson, "they'll file the report and let it gather dust for a thousand years or so."

"They can do anything they want," Decker told him. "We turn it in. What someone else does with it after that is their affair, not ours."

They sat quietly watching the six robots roll out the first of the packing cases, rip off its covers and unpack the seventh robot, laying out his various parts neatly in a row in the tramped-down, waist-high grass. Then, working as a team, with not a single fumble, they put No. 7 together, screwed his brain case into his metal skull, flipped up his energizing switch and slapped the breastplate home.

No. 7 stood groggily for a moment. He swung his arms uncertainly, shook his head from side to side. Then, having oriented himself, he stepped briskly forward and helped the other six heave the packing box containing No. 8 off the conveyor belt.

"Takes a little time this way," said Decker, "but it saves a lot of space. Have to cut our robot crew in half if we didn't pack them at the end of every job. They stow away better."

He sipped at his highball speculatively. Jackson lit a cigarette.

"Someday," said Jackson, "we're going to run up against something that we can't handle."

Decker snorted.

"Maybe here," insisted Jackson, gesturing at the nightmare jungle world outside the great curved sweep of the vision plate.

"You're a romanticist," Decker told him shortly. "In love with the unexpected. Besides that, you're new. Get a dozen trips under your belt and you won't feel this way."

"It could happen," insisted Jackson.

Decker nodded, almost sleepily. "Maybe," he said. "Maybe it could, at that. It never has, but I suppose it could. And when it does, we take it on the lam. It's no part of our job to fight a last ditch battle. When we bump up against something that's too big to handle, we don't stick around. We don't take any risks."

He took another sip. "Not even calculated risks," he added.

The ship rested on the top of a low hill, in a small

clearing masked by tall grass, sprinkled here and there with patches of exotic flowers. Below the hill a river flowed sluggishly, a broad expanse of chocolate-colored water moving in a sleepy tide through the immense vine-entangled forest.

As far as the eye could see, the jungle stretched away, a brooding darkness that even from behind the curving quartz of the vision plate seemed to exude a heady, musty scent of danger that swept up over the grass-covered hilltop. There was no sign of life, but one knew, almost instinctively, that sentiency lurked in the buried pathways and tunnels of the great tree-land.

Robot No. 8 had been energized, and now the eight, split into two groups, ran out two packing cases at a time instead of one. Soon there were twelve robots, and then they formed themselves into three working groups.

"Like that," said Decker, picking up the conversation where they had left it lying. He gestured with his glass, now empty. "No calculated risks. We send the robots first. They unpack and set up their fellows. Then the whole gang turns to and uncrates the machinery and sets it up and gets it operating. A man doesn't even put his foot on the ground until he has a steel ring around the ship to give him protection."

Jackson sighed. "I guess you're right," he said. "Nothing can happen. We don't take any chances. Not a single one."

"Why should we?" Decker asked. He heaved himself out of the chair, stood up and stretched. "Got a thing or two to do," he said. "Last minute checks and so on."

"I'll sit here for a while," said Jackson. "I like to watch. It's all new to me."

"You'll get over it," Decker told him. "In another twenty years."

In his office, Decker lifted a sheaf of preliminary reports off his desk and ran through them slowly, checking each one carefully, filing away in his mind the basic facts of the world outside.

He worked stolidly, wetting a big, blunt thumb against his outthrust tongue to flip the pages off the top of the next stack and deposit them, in not so neat a pile, to his right, face downward.

80

Atmosphere—pressure slightly more than Earth. High in oxygen. Gravity—a bit more than Earth. Temperature —hot. Jungle worlds always were. There was a breeze outside now, he thought. Maybe there'd be a breeze most of the time. That would be a help. Rotation—thirty-six hour day.

Radiation—none of local origin, but some hard stuff getting through from the sun. He made a mental note: Watch that.

Bacterial and virus count—as usual. Lots of it. Apparently not too dangerous. Not with every single soul hypoed and immunized and hormoned to his eyebrows. But you never can be sure, he thought. Not entirely sure. No calculated risks, he had told Jackson. But here was a calculated risk, and one you couldn't do a single thing about. If there was a bug that picked you for a host and you weren't loaded for bear to fight him, you took him on and did the best you could. Life factor—lot of emanation. Probably the vegetation, maybe even the soil, was crawling with all sorts of loathsome life. Vicious stuff, more than likely. But that was something you took care of as a matter of routine. No use taking any chances. You went over the ground even if there was no life— just to be sure there wasn't.

A tap came on the door and he called out for the man to enter.

It was Captain Carr, commander of the Legion unit.

Carr saluted snappily. Decker did not rise. He made his answering salute a sloppy one on purpose. No use, he told himself, letting the fellow establish any semblance of equality, for there was no such equality in fact. A captain of the Legion simply did not rank with the commandant of a galactic survey party.

"Reporting, sir," said Carr. "We are ready for a landing."

"Fine, Captain. Fine." What was the matter with the fool? The Legion always was ready, always would be ready—that was no more than tradition. Why, then, carry out such an empty, stiff formality?

But it was the nature of a man like Carr, he supposed. The Legion, with its rigid discipline, with its ancient pride of service and tradition, attracted men like Carr, was a perfect finishing school for accomplished martinets.

Tin soldiers, Decker thought, but accomplished ones. As hard-bitten a gang of fighting men as the galaxy had ever known. They were drilled and disciplined to a razor's edge, serum- and hormone-injected against all known diseases of an alien world, trained and educated in alien psychology and strictly indoctrinated with high survival characteristics which stood up under even the most adverse circumstances.

"We shall not be ready for some time, Captain," Decker said. "The robots have just started their uncrating."

"Very well," said Carr. "We await your orders, sir."

"Thank you, Captain," Decker told him, making it quite clear that he wished he would get out. But when Carr turned to go, Decker called him back.

"What is it, sir?" asked Carr.

"I've been wondering," said Decker. "Just wondering, you understand. Can you imagine any circumstances which might arise that the Legion could not handle?"

Carr's expression was a pure delight to see. "I'm afraid, sir, that I don't understand your question."

Decker sighed. "I didn't think you would," he said.

Before nightfall, the full working force of robots had been uncrated and had set up some of the machines, enough to establish a small circle of alarm posts around the ship.

A flame thrower burned a barren circle on the hilltop, stretching five hundred feet around the ship. A hard-radiations generator took up its painstaking task, pouring pure death into the soil. The toll must have been terrific. In some spots the ground virtually boiled as the dying life forms fought momentarily and fruitlessly to escape the death that cut them down.

The robots rigged up huge batteries of lamps that set the hilltop ablaze with a light as bright as day, and the work went on.

As yet, no human had set foot outside the ship.

Inside the ship, the robot stewards set up a table in the lounge so that the human diners might see what was going on outside the ship.

The entire company, except for the legionnaires who

82

stayed in quarters, had gathered for the meal when Decker came into the room.

"Good evening, gentlemen," he said.

He strode to the table's head and the others ranged themselves along the sides. He sat down and there was a scraping of drawn chairs as the others took their places.

He clasped his hands in front of him and bowed his head and parted his lips to say the customary words. He halted even as he was about to speak, and when the words did come they were different from the ones he had said by rote a thousand times before.

"Dear Father, we are Thy servants in an unknown land and there is a deadly pride upon us. Teach us humility and lead us to the knowledge, before it is too late, that men, despite their far traveling and their mighty works, still are as children in Thy sight. Bless the bread we are about to break, we beg Thee, and keep us forever in Thy compassion. Amen."

He lifted his head and looked down the table. Some of them, he saw, were startled. The others were amused.

They wonder if I'm cracking, he thought. They think the Old Man is breaking up. And that may be true, for all I know. Although I was all right until this afternoon. All right until young Doug Jackson . . .

"Those were fine words, lad," said Old MacDonald, the chief engineer. "I thank you for them, sir, and there is them among us who would do well to take some heed upon them."

Platters and plates were being passed up and down the table's length and there was the commonplace, homely clatter of silverware and china.

"This looks an interesting world," said Waldron, the anthropologist. "Dickson and I were up in observation just before the sun set. We thought we saw something down by the river. Some sort of life."

Decker grunted, scooping fried potatoes out of a bowl onto his plate. "Funny if we don't run across a lot of life here. The radiation wagon stirred up a lot of it when it went over the field today."

"What Waldron and I saw," said Dickson, "looked humanoid."

Decker squinted at the biologist. "Sure of that?" he asked.

83

Dickson shook his head. "The seeing was poor. Couldn't be absolutely sure. Seemed to me there were two or three of them. Matchstick men."

Waldron nodded. "Like a picture a kid would draw," he said. "One stroke for the body. Two strokes each for arms and legs. A circle for a head. Angular. Ungraceful. Skinny."

"Graceful enough in motion, though," said Dickson. "When they moved, they went like cats. Flowed, sort of."

"We'll know plenty soon enough," Decker told them mildly. "In a day or two we'll flush them."

Funny, he thought. On almost every job someone popped up to report he had spotted humanoids. Usually there weren't any. Usually it was just imagination. Probably wishful thinking, he told himself, the yen of men far away from their fellow men to find in an alien place a type of life that somehow seemed familiar.

Although the usual humanoid, once you met him in the flesh, turned out to be so repulsively alien that alongside him an octopus would seem positively human.

Franey, the senior geologist, said, "I've been thinking about those mountains to the west of us, the ones we caught sight of when we were coming in. Had a new look about them. New mountains are good to work in. They haven't worn down. Easier to get at whatever's in them."

"We'll lay out our first survey lines in that direction," Decker told him.

Outside the curving vision plate, the night was alive with the blaze of the batteries of lights. Gleaming robots toiled in shining gangs. Ponderous machines lumbered past. Smaller ones scurried like frightened beetles. To the south, great gouts of flame leaped out, and the sky was painted red with the bursts of a squad of flame throwers going into action.

"Chewing out a landing field," said Decker. "A tongue of jungle juts out there. Absolutely level ground. Like a floor. Won't take a great deal of work to turn it into a field."

The stewards brought coffee and brandy and a box of good cigars. Decker and his men settled back into their chairs, taking life easy, watching the work going on outside the ship.

"I hate this waiting," Franey said, settling down comfortably to his cigar.

"Part of the job," said Decker. He poured more brandy into his coffee.

By dawn the last machines were set up and had either been moved out to their assigned positions or were parked in the motor pool. The flamers had enlarged the burned-over area and three radiation wagons were busy on their rounds. To the south, the airfield had been finished and the jets were lined up and waiting in a plumb-straight row.

Some of the robots, their work done for the moment, formed themselves in solid ranks to form a solid square, neat and orderly and occupying a minimum of space. They stood there in the square, waiting against the time when they would be needed, a motor pool of robots, a reservoir of manpower.

Finally the gangplank came down and the legionnaires marched out in files of two, with clank and glitter and a remorseless precision that put machines to shame. There were no banners and there were no drums, for these are useless things and the Legion, despite its clank and glitter, was an organization of ruthless efficiency.

The column wheeled and became a line, and the line broke up and the platoons moved out toward the planethead perimeter. There machines and legionnaires and robots manned the frontier that Earth had set up on an alien world.

Busy robots staked out and set up an open-air pavilion of gaudily striped canvas that rippled in the breeze, placed tables and chairs beneath its shade, moved in a refrigerator filled with beer and with extra ice compartments.

At last it was safe and comfortable for ordinary men to leave the shelter of the ship.

Organization, Decker told himself—organization and efficiency and leaving not a thing to chance. Plug every loophole before it becomes a loophole. Crush possible resistance before it develops as resistance. Gain absolute control over a certain number of square feet of planet and operate from there.

Later, of course, there were certain chances taken; you just couldn't eliminate them all. There would be field trips, and even with all the precautions that robot and

85

machine and legionnaire could offer there would be certain risks. There would be aerial survey and mapping, and these, too, would have elements of chance, but with these elements reduced to the very minimum.

And always there would be the base, an absolutely safe and impregnable base to which a field party or a survey flight could retreat, from which reinforcements could be sent out or counteraction taken.

Foolproof, he told himself. As foolproof as it could be made.

He wondered briefly what had been the matter with him the night before. It had been that young fool, Jackson, of course—a capable biochemist, possibly, but certainly the wrong kind of man for a job like this. Something had slipped up: the screening board should have stopped a man like Jackson, should have spotted his emotional instability. Not that he could do any actual harm, of course, but he could be upsetting. An irritant, thought Decker, that is what he is. Just an irritant.

Decker laid an armload of paraphernalia on the long table underneath the gay pavilion. From it he selected a rolled-up sheet of map paper, unrolled it, spread it flat and thumb-tacked it at four corners. On it a portion of the river and the mountains to the west had been roughly penciled in. The base was represented by an X'ed-through square—but the rest of it was blank.

But it would be filled in—as the days went by it would take shape and form.

From the field to the south a jet whooshed into the sky, made a lazy turn and straightened out to streak toward the west. Decker walked to the edge of the pavilion's shade and watched it as it dwindled out of sight. That would be Jarvis and Donnelly, assigned to the preliminary survey of the southwest sector between the base and the western mountains.

Another jet rose lazily, trailing its column of exhaust, gathered speed and sprang into the sky. Freeman and Johns, he thought.

Decker went back to the table, pulled out a chair and sat down. He picked up a pencil and tapped it idly on the almost-blank map paper. Behind his back he heard another jet whoom upward from the field.

He let his eyes take in the base. Already it was losing

its raw, burned-over look. Already it had something of the look of Earth about it, of the efficiency and common sense and get-the-job-done attitude of the men of Earth.

Small groups of men stood around talking. One of them, he saw, squatted on the ground, talking something over with three squatting robots. Others walked around, sizing up the situation.

Decker grunted with satisfaction. A capable gang of men, he thought. Most of them would have to wait around to really get down to work until the first surveys came in, but even while they waited they would not be idle.

They'd take soil samples and test them. The life that swarmed in the soil would be captured and brought in by grinning robots, and the squirming, vicious things would be pinned down and investigated—photographed, X-rayed, dissected, analyzed, observed, put through re-action tests. Trees and plants and grasses would be catalogued and attempts made to classify them. Test pits would be dug for a look at soil strata. The river's water would be analyzed. Seines would dredge up some of the life they held. Wells would be driven to establish water tables.

All of this here, at the moment, while they waited for the first preliminary flights to bring back data that would pin-point other areas worthy of investigation.

Once those reports were in, the work would be started in dead earnest. Geologists and mineral men would probe into the planet's hide. Weather observation points would be set up. Botanists would take far-ranging check samples. Each man would do the work for which he had been trained. Field reports would pour back to the base, there to be correlated and fitted into the picture.

Work then, work in plenty. Work by day and night. And all the time the base would be a bit of Earth, a few square yards held inviolate against all another world might muster.

Decker sat easily in his chair and felt the breeze that came beneath the canvas, a gentle breeze that ruffled through his hair, rattled the papers on the table and twitched the tacked-down map. It was pleasant here, he thought. But it wouldn't stay pleasant long. It almost never did.

Someday, he thought, I'll find a pleasant planet, a paradise planet where the weather's always perfect and there is food for the picking of it and natives that are intelligent to talk with and companionable in other ways, and I will never leave it. I'll refuse to leave when the ship is ready to blast off. I'll live out my days in a fascinating corner of a lousy galaxy—a galaxy that is gaunt with hunger and mad with savagery and lonely beyond all that may be said of loneliness.

He looked up from his reverie and saw Jackson standing at the pavilion's edge, watching him.

"What's the matter, Jackson?" Decker asked with sudden bitterness. "Why aren't you—"

"They're bringing in a native, sir," said Jackson, breathlessly. "One of the things Waldron and Dickson saw."

The native was humanoid, but he was not human.

As Waldron and Dickson had said, he was a matchstick man, a flesh and blood extension of a drawing a four-year-old might make. He was black as the ace of spades, and he wore no clothing, but the eyes that looked out of the pumpkin-shaped head at Decker were bright with a light that might have been intelligence.

Decker tensed as he looked into those eyes. Then he looked away and saw the men standing silently around the pavilion's edge, silent and waiting, tense as he was.

Slowly Decker reached out his hand to one of the two headsets of the mentograph. His fingers closed over it and for a moment he felt a vague, but forceful, reluctance to put it on his head. It was disturbing to contact, or attempt to contact, an alien mind. It gave one a queasy feeling in the pit of the stomach. It was a thing, he thought, that Man never had been intended to do—an experience that was utterly foreign to any human background.

He lifted the headset slowly, fitted it over his skull, made a sign toward the second set.

For a long moment the alien eyes watched him, the creature standing erect and motionless.

Courage, thought Decker. Raw and naked courage, to stand there in this suddenly unfamiliar environment that had blossomed almost overnight on familiar ground, to stand there motionless and erect, surrounded by creatures that must look as if they had dropped from some horrible nightmare.

The humanoid took one step closer to the table, reached out a hand and took the headset. Fumbling with its unfamiliarity, he clamped it on his head. And never for a moment did the eyes waver from Decker's eyes, always alert and watchful.

Decker forced himself to relax, tried to force his mind into an attitude of peace and calm. That was a thing you had to be careful of. You couldn't scare these creatures—you had to lull them, quiet them down, make them feel your friendliness. They would be upset, and a sudden thought, even a suggestion of human brusqueness would wind them up tighter than a drum.

There was intelligence here, he told himself, being careful to keep his mind unruffled, a greater intelligence than one would think, looking at the creature. Intelligence enough to know that he should put on the headset, and guts enough to do it.

He caught the first faint mental whiff of the matchstick man, and the pit of his stomach contracted suddenly and there was an ache around his chest. There was nothing in the thing he caught, nothing that could be put into words, but there was an alienness, as a smell is alien. There was a non-human connotation that set one's teeth on edge. He fought back the gagging blackness of repulsive disgust that sought to break the smooth friendliness he held within his mind.

"We are friendly," Decker forced himself to think. "We are friendly. We are friendly. We are friendly. We are friendly. We are—"

"You should not have come," said the thought of the matchstick man.

"We will not harm you," Decker thought. "We are friendly. We will not harm you. We will not harm—"

"You will never leave," said the humanoid.

"Let us be friends," thought Decker. "Let us be friends. We have gifts. We will help you. We will—"

"You should not have come," said the matchstick thought. "But since you are here, you can never leave."

Humor him, thought Decker to himself. Humor him.

"All right, then," he thought. "We will stay. We will

stay and we will be friendly. We will stay and teach you. We will give you the things we have brought for you and we will stay with you."

"You will not leave," said the matchstick man's thought, and there was something so cold and logical and matter-of-fact about the way the thought was delivered that Decker suddenly was cold.

The humanoid meant it—meant every word he said. He was not being dramatic, nor was he blustering—but neither was he bluffing. He actually thought that the humans would not leave, that they would not live to leave the planet. Decker smiled softly to himself.

"You will die here," said the humanoid thought.

"Die?" asked Decker. "What is die?"

The matchstick man's thought was pure disgust. Deliberately he reached up, took off the headset and laid it carefully back upon the table. Then he turned and walked away, and not a man made a move to stop him.

Decker took off his headset and slammed it on the table top.

"Jackson," he said, "pick up that phone and tell the Legion to let him through. Let him leave. Don't try to stop him."

He sat limply in his chair and looked at the ring of faces that were watching him.

Waldron asked, "What is it, Decker?"

"He sentenced us to death," said Decker. "He said that we would not leave the planet. He said that we would die here."

"Strong words," said Waldron.

"He meant them," Decker said.

He lifted a hand, flipped it wearily. "He doesn't know, of course," he said. "He really thinks that he can stop us from leaving. He thinks that we will die."

It was an amusing situation, really. That a naked humanoid should walk out of the jungle and threaten to do away with a human survey party, that he should really think that he could do it. That he should be so positive about it.

But there was not a single smile on any of the faces that looked at Decker.

"We can't let it get us," Decker said.

"Nevertheless," Waldron declared, "we should take precautions."

Decker nodded. "We'll go on emergency alert immediately," he said. "We'll stay that way until we're sure . . . until we're . . ." His voice trailed off. Sure of what? Sure that an alien savage who wore no clothing, who had not a sign of culture about him, could wipe out a group of humans protected by a ring of steel, held wihin a guard of machines and robots and a group of fighting men who knew all there was to know concerning the refinements of dealing out swift and merciless extermination to anything that moved against them?

Ridiculous!

Of course it was ridiculous! And yet the eyes had held intelligence. The being had not only intelligence but courage. He had stood within a circle of to him—alien beings, and he had not flinched. He had faced the unknown and said what there was to say, and then had walked away with a dignity any human would have been proud to wear. He must have guessed that the alien beings within the confines of the base were not of his own planet, for he had said that they should not have come, and his thought had implied that he was aware they were not of this world of his. He had understood that he was supposed to put on the headset, but whether that was an act more of courage than of intelligence one would never know—for you could not know if he had realized what the headset had been for. Not knowing, the naked courage of clamping it to his head was of an order that could not be measured.

"What do you think?" Decker asked Waldron.

"We'll have to be careful," Waldron told him evenly. "We'll have to watch our step. Take all precautions, now that we are warned. But there's nothing to be scared of, nothing we can't handle."

"He was bluffing," Dickson said. "Trying to scare us into leaving."

Decker shook his head. "I don't think he was," he said, "I tried to bluff him and it didn't work. He's just as sure as we are."

The work went on. There was no attack.

The jets roared out and thrummed away, mapping the

land. Field parties went out cautiously. They were flanked by robots and by legionnaires and preceded by lumbering machines that knifed and tore and burned a roadway through even the most stubborn of the terrain they went up against. Radio weather stations were set up at distant points, and at the base the weather tabulators clicked off on tape the data that the stations sent back.

Other field parties were flown into the special areas pinpointed for more extensive exploration and investigation.

And nothing happened.

The days went past. The weeks went past. The machines and robots watched, and the legionnaires stood ready, and the men hurried with their work so they could get off the planet.

A bed of coal was found and mapped. An iron range was discovered. One area in the mountains to the west crawled with radioactive ores. The botanists found twenty-seven species of edible fruit. The base swarmed with animals that had been trapped as specimens and remained as pets.

And a village of the matchstick men was found. It wasn't much of a place. Its huts were primitive. Its sanitation was nonexistent. Its people were peaceful.

Decker left his chair under the striped pavilion to lead a party to the village.

The party entered cautiously, weapons ready, but being very careful not to move too fast, not to speak too quickly, not to make a motion that might be construed as hostile.

The natives sat in their doorways and watched them. They did not speak and they scarcely moved a muscle. They simply watched the humans as they marched to the center of the village.

There the robots set up a table and placed a mentograph upon it. Decker sat down in a chair and put one of the headsets on his skull. The rest of the party waited off to one side. Decker waited at the table.

They waited for an hour and not a native stirred. None came forward to put on the other headset.

Decker took off the headset wearily and placed it on the table.

"It's no use," he said. "It won't work. Go ahead and

92

take your pictures. Do anything you wish. But don't disturb the natives. Don't touch a single thing."

He took a handkerchief out of his pocket and mopped his steaming face.

Waldron came and leaned on the table. "What do you make of it?" he asked.

Decker shook his head. "It haunts me," he said. "There's just one thing that I am thinking. It must be wrong. It can't be right. But the thought came to me, and I can't get rid of it."

"Sometimes that happens," Waldron said. "No matter how illogical a thing may be, it sticks with a man, like a burr inside his brain."

"The thought is this," said Decker. "That they have told us all they have to tell us. That they have nothing more they wish to say to us."

"That's what you thought," said Waldron.

Decker nodded. "A funny thing to think," he said. "Out of a clear sky. And it can't be right."

"I don't know," said Waldron. "Nothing's right here. Notice that they haven't got a single iron tool. Not a scrap of metal in evidence at all. Their cooking utensils are stone, a sort of funny stuff like soapstone. What few tools they have are stone. And yet they have a culture. And they have it without metal."

"They're intelligent," said Decker. "Look at them watching us. Not afraid. Just waiting. Calm and sure of themselves. And that fellow who came into the base. He knew what to do with the headset."

Waldron sucked thoughtfully at a tooth. "We'd better be getting back to base," he said. "It's getting late." He held his wrist in front of him. "My watch has stopped. What time do you have, Decker?"

Decker lifted his arm and Waldron heard the sharp gasp of his indrawn breath. Slowly Decker raised his head and looked at the other man.

"My watch has stopped, too," he said, and his voice was scarcely louder than a whisper.

For a moment they were graven images, shocked into immobility by a thing that should have been no more than an inconvenience. Then Waldron sprang erect from the table, whirled to face the men and robots.

"Assemble!" he shouted. "Back to the base. Quick!"

The men came running. The robots fell into place. The column marched away. The natives sat quietly in their doorways and watched them as they left.

Decker sat in his camp chair and listened to the canvas of the pavilion snapping softly in the wind, alive in the wind, talking and laughing to itself. A lantern, hung on a ring above his head, swayed gently, casting fleeting shadows that seemed at times to be the shadows of living, moving things. A robot stood stiffly and quietly beside one of the pavilion poles.

Stolidly, Decker reached out a finger and stirred the little pile of wheels and springs that lay upon the table.

Sinister, he thought. Sinister and queer.

The guts of watches, lying on the table. Not of two watches alone, not only his and Waldron's watches, but many other watches from the wrists of other men. All of them silent, stilled in their task of marking time.

Night had fallen hours before, but the base still was astir with activity that was at once feverish and furtive. Men moved about in the shadows and crossed the glaring patches of brilliance shed by the batteries of lights set up by the robots many weeks before. Watching the men, one would have sensed that they moved with a haunting sense of doom, would have known as well that they knew, deep in their inmost hearts, that there was no doom to fear. No definite thing that one could put a finger on and say, this is the thing to fear. No direction that one might point toward and say, doom lies here, waiting to spring upon us.

Just one small thing.

Watches had stopped running. And that was a simple thing for which there must be some simple explanation.

Except, thought Decker, on an alien planet no occurrence, no accident or incident, can be regarded as a simple thing for which a simple explanation must necessarily be anticipated. For the matrix of cause and effect, the mathematics of chance, may not hold true on an alien planet as they hold true on Earth.

There was one rule, Decker thought grimly. One rule: Take no chances. That was the one safe rule to follow, the only rule to follow.

Following it, he had ordered all field parties back to

94

base, had ordered the crew to prepare the ship for emergency take-off, had alerted the robots to be ready at an instant to get the machines aboard. Even to be prepared to desert the machines and leave without them if circumstances should dictate that this was necessary.

Having done that, there was no more to do but wait. Wait until the field parties came back from their advance camps. Wait until some reason could be assigned to the failure of the watches.

It was not a thing, he told himself, that should be allowed to panic one. It was something to recognize, not to disregard. It was a circumstance that made necessary a certain number of precautions, but it was not a situation that should make one lose all sense of proportion.

You could not go back to Earth and say, "Well, you see, our watches stopped and so . . ."

A footstep sounded and he swung around in his chair. It was Jackson.

"What is it, Jackson?" Decker asked.

"The camps aren't answering, sir," said Jackson. "The operator has been trying to raise them and there is no answer. Not a single peep."

Decker grunted. "Take it easy," he said. "They will answer. Give them time."

He wished, even as he spoke, that he could feel some of the assurance that he tried to put into his voice. For a second, a rising terror mounted in his throat and he choked it back.

"Sit down," he said. "We'll sit here and have a beer and then we'll go down to the radio shack and see what's doing."

He rapped on the table. "Beer," he said. "Two beers."

The robot standing by the pavilion pole did not answer.

He made his voice louder. The robot did not stir.

Decker put his clenched fists upon the table and tried to rise, but his legs were suddenly cold and had turned unaccountably to water, and he could not raise himself.

"Jackson," he panted, "go and tap that robot on the shoulder. Tell him we want beer."

He saw the fear that whitened Jackson's face as he rose and moved slowly forward. Inside himself he felt the terror start and worry at his throat.

Jackson stood beside the robot and reached out a hesitant hand, tapped him gently on the shoulder, tapped him harder—and the robot fell flat upon its face!

Feet hammered across the hard-packed ground, heading for the pavilion.

Decker jerked himself around, sat foursquare and solid in his chair, waiting for the man who ran.

It was MacDonald, the chief engineer.

He halted in front of Decker and his hands, scarred and grimy with years of fighting balky engines, reached down and gripped the boards of the table's edge. His seamy face was twisted as if he were about to weep.

"The ship, sir. The ship . . ."

Decker nodded, almost idly. "I know, Mr. MacDonald. The ship won't run."

MacDonald gulped. "The big stuff's all right, sir. But the little gadgets . . . the injector mechanism . . . the—"

He stopped abruptly and stared at Decker. "You knew," he said. "How did you know?"

"I knew," said Decker, "that someday it would come. Not like this, perhaps. But in any one of several ways. I knew that the day would come when our luck would run too thin. I talked big, like the rest of you, of course, but I knew that it would come. The day when we'd covered all the possibilities but the one that we could not suspect, and that, of course, would be the one that would ruin us."

He was thinking, the natives had no metal. No sign of any metal in their village at all. Their dishes were soapstone, and they wore no ornaments. Their implements were stone. And yet they were intelligent enough, civilized enough, cultured enough to have fabricated metal. For there was metal here, a great deposit of it in the western mountains. They had tried perhaps, many centuries ago, had fashioned metal tools and had them go to pieces underneath their fingers in a few short weeks.

A civilization without metal. A culture without metal. It was unthinkable. Take metal from a man and he went back to the caves. Take metal from a man and he was earthbound, and his bare hands were all he had.

Waldron came into the pavilion, walking quietly in the silence. "The radio is dead," he said, "and the robots

96

are dying like flies. The place is littered with them, just so much scrap metal."

Decker nodded. "The little stuff, the finely fabricated, will go first," he said. "Like watches and radio innards and robot brains and injector mechanisms. Next, the generators will go and we will have no lights or power. Then the machines will break down and the Legion's weapons will be no more than clubs. After that, the big stuff, probably."

"The native told us," Waldron said, "when you talked to him. 'You will never leave,' he said."

"We didn't understand," said Decker. "We thought he was threatening us and we knew that we were too big, too well guarded for any threat of his to harm us. He wasn't threatening us at all, of course. He was just telling us."

He made a hopeless gesture with his hands. "What is it?"

"No one knows," said Waldron quietly. "Not yet, at least. Later we may find out, but it won't help us any. A microbe, maybe. A virus. Something that eats iron after it has been subjected to heat or alloyed with other metals. It doesn't go for iron ore. If it did, that deposit we found would have been gone long ago."

"If that is true," said Decker, "we've brought it the first square meal it's had in a long, long time. A thousand years. Maybe a million years. There is no fabricated metal here. How would it survive? Without stuff to eat, how would it live?"

"I wouldn't know," said Waldron. "It might not be a metal-eating organism at all. It might be something else. Something in the atmosphere."

"We tested the atmosphere." But, even as the words left his mouth, Decker saw how foolish they were. They had tested the atmosphere, but how could they have detected something they had never run across before? Man's yardstick was limited—limited to the things he knew about, limited by the circle of his own experience. He guarded himself against the obvious and the imaginable. He could not guard himself against the unknowable or the unimaginable.

Decker rose and saw Jackson still standing by the pavilion pole, with the robot stretched at his feet.

"You have your answer," he told the biochemist. "Remember that first day here? You talked with me in the lounge."

Jackson nodded. "I remember, sir."

And suddenly, Decker realized, the entire base was quiet.

A gust of wind came out of the jungle and rattled the canvas.

Now, for the first time since they had landed, he caught in the wind the alien smell of an alien world.

THE ANSWERS

I

THEY knew it when they stepped out of the ship and saw it. There was, of course, no way that they could have known it, or have been sure they knew it, for there was no way to know what one might be looking for. Yet they did know it for what it was, and three of them stood and looked at it and the fourth one floated and looked at it. And each of them, in his brain or heart or intuition, whatever you may name it, knew deep inside himself a strange conviction that here finally was the resting place, or one of the resting places, of that legendary fragment of the human race that millenia before had broken free of the chains of ordinary humans to make their way into the darkness of the outer galaxy. But whether they had fled from mediocrity or whether they had deserted or whether they had left for any one of a dozen other reasons was a thing that no one now might know, for the matter had become an academic question that had split into several cults of erudite belief and still was fiercely debated in a very learned manner.

In the minds of the four who looked, however, there was no shred of question that here before them lay the place that had been sought, in a more or less haphazard fashion, for a hundred thousand years. It was a place. One hesitated to call it a city, although it probably was a city. It was a place of living and of learning and of working and it had many buildings, but the buildings had been made a part of the landscape and did not outrage the eye with their grossness or their disregard for the land they stood upon. There was greatness about the place—not the greatness of gigantic stones heaped on one another, nor the greatness of a bold and overwhelming architecture, nor even the greatness of indestructibility. For there was no massiveness of structure and the architecture seemed quite ordinary, and some of the buildings had fallen into disrepair and others were weathered into a mellowness that blended with the trees and grass of the hills on which they stood.

Still, there was a greatness in them, the greatness of humility and purpose and the greatness, too, of well-ordered life. Looking at them, one knew that he had been wrong in thinking this a city—that this was no city, but an extensive village, with all the connotations that were in the word.

But most of all there was humanness, the subtle touch that marked the buildings as those that had been planned by human minds and raised by human hands. You could not put your finger upon any single thing and say, this thing is human, for any one thing you put your finger on might have been built or achieved by another race. But when all those single things were rolled into the whole concept there could be no doubt that it was a human village.

Sentient beings had hunted for this place, had sought the clue that might lead them to the vanished segment of the race, and when they failed, some of them had doubted there had been such a place, with the records that told of it often in dispute. There were those, too, who had said that it mattered little whether you found the missing fragment or not, since little that was of any value would come from a race so insignificant as the human race. What were the humans? they would ask you and would answer before you had a chance to speak. Gadgeteers, they said, gadgeteers who were singularly unstable. Great on gadgets, they would say, but with very little real intelligence. It was, they would point out, only by the slightest margin of intelligence that they were ever accepted into the galactic brotherhood. And, these detractors would remind you, they had not improved much since. Still marvelous gadgeteers, of course, but strictly third-rate citizens who now quite rightly had been relegated to the backwash of the empire.

The place had been sought, and there had been many failures. It had been sought, but not consistently, for there were matters of much greater import than finding it. It was simply an amusing piece of galactic history, or myth, if you would rather. As a project, its discovery had never rated very high.

But here it was, spread out below the high ridge on which the ship had landed, and if any of them wondered why it had not been found before, there was a simple answer—there were just too many stars; you could not search them all.

"This is it," said the Dog, speaking in his mind, and he looked slantwise at the Human, wondering what the Human might be thinking, for, of all of them, the finding of this place must mean the most to him.

"I am glad we found it," said the Dog, speaking directly to the Human, and the Human caught the nuances of the thought, the closeness of the Dog and his great compassion and his brotherhood.

"Now we shall know," the Spider said, and each of them knew, without actually saying so, that now they'd know if these humans were any different from the other humans, or if they were just the same old humdrum race.

"They were mutants," said the Globe, "or they were supposed to be."

The Human stood there, saying nothing, just looking at the place.

"If we'd tried to find it," said the Dog, "we never would have done it."

"We can't spend much time," the Spider told them. "Just a quick survey, then there's this other business."

"The point is," said the Globe, "we know that it exists and where it is. They will send experts out to investigate."

"We stumbled on it," said the Human, half in wonderment. "We just stumbled on it."

The Spider made a thought that sounded like a chuckle and the Human said no more.

"It's deserted," said the Globe. "They have run away again."

"They may be decadent," said the Spider. "We may find

what's left of them huddled in some corner, wondering what it's all about, loaded down with legends and with crazy superstitions."

"I don't think so," said the Dog.

"We can't spend much time," the Spider said again.

"We should spend no time at all," the Globe told them. "We were not sent out to find this place. We have no business letting it delay us."

"Since we've found it," said the Dog, "it would be a shame to go away and leave it, just like that."

"Then let's get at it," said the Spider. "Let's break out the robots and the ground car."

"If you don't mind," the Human said, "I think that I will walk. The rest of you go ahead. I'll just walk down and take a look around."

"I'll go with you," said the Dog.

"I thank you," said the Human, "but there really is no need."

So they let him go alone.

The three of them stayed on the ridge top and watched him walk down the hill toward the silent buildings.

Then they went to activate the robots.

The sun was setting when they returned, and the Human was waiting for them, squatting on the ridge, staring at the village.

He did not ask them what they had found. It was almost as if he knew, although he could not have found the answer by himself, just walking around.

They told him.

The Dog was kind about it. "It's strange," he said. "There is no evidence of any great development. No hint of anything unusual. In fact, you might guess that they had retrogressed. There are no great engines, no hint of any mechanical ability."

"There are gadgets," said the Human. "Gadgets of comfort and convenience. That is all I saw."

"That is all there is," the Spider said.

"There are no humans," said the Globe. "No life of any kind. No intelligence."

"The experts," said the Dog, "may find something when they come."

"I doubt it," said the Spider.

The Human turned his head away from the village and

looked at his three companions. The Dog was sorry, of course, that they had found so little, sorry that the little they had found had been so negative. The Dog was sorry because he still held within himself some measure of racial memory and of loyalty. The old associations with the human race had been wiped away millenia ago, but the heritage still held, the old heritage of sympathy with and for the being that had walked with his ancestors so understandingly.

The Spider was almost pleased about it, pleased that he had found no evidence of greatness, that this last vestige of vanity that might be held by humans now would be dashed forever and the race must now slink back into its corner and stay there, watching with furtive eyes the greatness of the Spiders and the other races.

The Globe didn't care. As he floated there, at head level with the Spider and the Dog, it meant little to him whether humans might be proud or humble. Nothing mattered to the Globe except that certain plans went forward, that certain goals were reached, that progress could be measured. Already the Globe had written off this village, already he had erased the story of the mutant humans as a factor that might affect progress, one way or another.

"I think," the Human said, "that I will stay out here for a while. That is, if you don't mind."

"We don't mind," the Globe told him.

"It will be getting dark," the Spider said.

"There'll be stars," the Human said. "There may even be a moon. Did you notice if there was a moon?"

"No," the Spider said.

"We'll be leaving soon," the Dog said to the Human. "I will come out and tell you when we have to leave."

There were stars, of course. They came out when the last flush of the sun still flamed along the west. First there were but a few of the brighter ones and then there were more, and finally the entire heaven was a network of unfamiliar stars. But there was no moon. Or, if there was one, it did not show itself.

Chill crept across the ridge and the Human found some sticks of wood lying about, dead branches and shriveled bushes and other wood that looked as if it might at one time have been milled and worked, and built himself a fire. It was a small fire but it flamed brightly in the darkness, and he huddled close against it, more for its companionship than for any heat it gave.

He sat beside it and looked down upon the village and told himself there was something wrong. The greatness of the human race, he told himself, could not have gone so utterly to seed. He was lonely, lonely with a throat-aching loneliness that was more than the loneliness of an alien planet and a chilly ridge and unfamiliar stars. He was lonely for the hope that once had glowed so brightly, for the promise that had gone like dust into nothingness before a morning wind, for a race that huddled in its gadgetry in the backwash of the empire.

Not an empire of humanity, but an empire of Globes and Spiders, of Dogs and other things for which there was scarcely a description.

There was more to the human race than gadgetry. There was destiny somewhere and the gadgetry was simply the means to bridge the time until that destiny should become apparent. In a fight for survival, he told himself, gadgetry might be the expedient, but it could not be the answer; it could not be the sum total, the final jotting down of any group of beings.

The Dog came and stood beside him without saying anything. He simply stood there and looked down with the Human at the quiet village that had been quiet so long, and the firelight flamed along his coat, and he was a thing of beauty with a certain inherent wildness still existing in him.

Finally the Dog broke the silence that hung above the world and seemed a part of it.

"The fire is nice," he said. "I seldom have a fire."

"The fire was first," the Human said. "The first step up. Fire is a symbol to me."

"I have symbols, too," the Dog said, gravely. "Even the Spider has some symbols. But the Globe has none."

"I feel sorry for the Globe," the Human said.

"Don't let your pity wear you down," the Dog told him. "The Globe feels sorry for you. He is sorry for all of us, for everything that is not a Globe."

"Once my people were sorry like that, too," the Human said. "But not any more."

"It's time to go," the Dog said. "I know you would like to stay, but . . ."

"I am staying," said the Human.

"You can't stay," the Dog told him.

"I am staying," the Human said. "I am just a Human and you can get along without me."

"I thought you would be staying," said the Dog. "Do you want me to go back and get your stuff?"

"If you would be so kind," the Human said. "I'd not like to go myself."

"The Globe will be angry," said the Dog.

"I know it."

"You will be demoted," said the Dog. "It will be a long time before you're allowed to go on a first class run again."

"I know all that."

"The Spider will say that all humans are crazy. He will say it in a very nasty way."

"I don't care," the Human said. "Somehow, I don't care."

"All right, then," said the Dog. "I will go and get your stuff. There are some books and your clothes and that little trunk of yours."

"And food," the Human said.

"Yes," declared the Dog. "I would not have forgotten food."

After the ship was gone the Human picked up the bundles the Dog had brought, and, in addition to all the Human's food, the Human saw that the Dog had left him some of his own as well.

II

The people of the village had lived a simple and a comfortable life. Much of the comfort paraphernalia had broken down and all of it had long since ceased to operate, but it was not hard for one to figure out what each of the gadgets did or once had been designed to do.

They had had a love of beauty, for there still were ruins of their gardens left, and here and there one found a flower or a flowering shrub that once had been tended carefully for its color and its grace; but these things had been long forgotten and had lost the grandeur of their

104

purpose, so that the beauty they now held was bittersweet and faded.

The people had been literate, for there were rows of books upon the shelves. The books went to dust when they were touched, and one could do no more than wonder at the magic words they held.

There were buildings which at one time might have been theaters and there were great forums where the populace might have gathered to hear the wisdom or the argument that was the topic of the day.

And even yet one could sense the peace and leisure, the order and the happiness that the place had once held.

There was no greatness. There were no mighty engines, nor the shops to make them. There were no launching platforms and no other hint that the dwellers in the village had ever dreamed of going to the stars, although they must have known about the stars since their ancestors had come from space. There were no defenses, and there were no great roads leading from the village into the outer planet.

One felt peace when he walked along the street, but it was a haunted peace, a peace that balanced on a knife's edge, and while one wished with all his heart that he could give way to it and live with it, one was afraid to do so for fear of what might happen.

The Human slept in the homes, clearing away the dust and the fallen debris, building tiny fires to keep him company. He sat outside, on the broken flagstones or the shattered bench, before he went to sleep, and stared up at the stars and thought how once those stars had made familiar patterns for a happy people. He wandered in the winding paths that were narrower now than they once had been and hunted for a clue, although he did not hunt too strenuously, for there was something here that said you should not hurry and you should not fret, for there was no purpose in it.

Here once had lain the hope of the human race, a mutant branch of that race that had been greater than the basic race. Here had been the hope of greatness and there was no greatness. Here were peace and comfort and intelligence and leisure, but nothing else that made itself apparent to the eye.

Although there must be something else, some lesson, some message, some purpose. The Human told himself again and again that this could not be a dead end, that it was more than some blind alley.

On the fifth day, in the center of the village, he found the building that was a little more ornate and somewhat more solidly built, although all the rest were solid enough for all conscience's sake. There were no windows and the single door was locked, and he knew at last that he had found the clue he had been hunting for.

He worked for three days to break into the building but there was no way that he could. On the fourth day he gave up and walked away, out of the village and across the hills, looking for some thought or some idea that might gain him entry to the building. He walked across the hills as one will pace his study when he is at a loss for words, or take a turn in the garden to clear his head for thinking.

And that is how he found the people.

First of all, he saw the smoke coming from one of the hollows that branched down toward the valley where a river ran, a streak of gleaming silver against the green of pasture grass.

He walked cautiously, so that he would not be surprised, but, strangely, without the slightest fear, for there was something in this planet, something in the arching sky and the song of bird and the way the wind blew out of the west that told a man he had not a thing to fear.

Then he saw the house beneath the mighty trees. He saw the orchard and the trees bending with their fruit and heard the thoughts of people talking back and forth.

He walked down the hill toward the house, not hurrying, for suddenly it had come upon him that there was no need to hurry. And, just as suddenly, it seemed that he was coming home, although that was the strangest thing of all, for he had never known a home that resembled this.

They saw him coming when he strode down across the orchard, but they did not rise and come to meet him. They sat where they were and waited, as if he were already a friend of theirs and his coming were expected.

There was an old lady with snow-white hair and a prim, neat dress, its collar coming up high at her throat to hide the ravages of age upon the human body. But her face was beautiful, the restful beauty of the very old, who sit and rock and know their day is done and that their life is full and that it has been good.

There was a man of middle age or more, who sat beside the woman. The sun had burned his face and neck until they were almost black, and his hands were calloused and pock-marked with old scars and half crippled with heavy work. But upon his face, too, was a calmness which was an incomplete reflection of the face beside him, incomplete because it was not so deep and settled, because it could not as yet know the full comfort of old age.

The third one was a young woman and the Human saw the calmness in her, too. She looked back at him out of cool gray eyes and he saw that her face was curved and soft and that she was much younger than he had first thought.

He stopped at the gate and the man rose and came to where he waited.

"You're welcome, stranger," said the man. "We heard you coming since you stepped into the orchard."

"I have been at the village," the Human said. "I am just out for a walk."

"You are from outside?"

"Yes," the Human told him, "I am from outside. My name is David Grahame."

"Come in, David," said the man, opening the gate. "Come and rest with us. There will be food and we have an extra bed."

He walked along the garden path with the man and came to the bench where the old lady sat.

"My name is Jed," the man said, "and this is my mother, Mary, and the other of us is my daughter Alice."

"So you finally came to us, young man," the old lady said to David.

She patted the bench with a fragile hand. "Here, sit down beside me and let us talk awhile. Jed has chores to do and Alice will have to cook the supper. But I am old and lazy and I only sit and talk."

Now that she talked, her eyes were brighter, but the calmness was still in them.

"We knew you would come someday," she said. "We

knew someone would come. For surely those who are outside would hunt their mutant kin."

"We found you," David said, "quite by accident."

"We? There are others of you?"

"The others went away. They were not human and they were not interested."

"But you stayed," she said. "You thought there would be things to find. Great secrets to be learned."

"I stayed," said David, "because I had to stay."

"But the secrets? The glory and the power?"

David shook his head. "I don't think I thought of that. Not of power and glory. But there must be something else. You sense it walking in the village and looking in the homes. You sense a certain truth."

"Truth," the old lady said. "Yes, we found the Truth."

And the way she said it Truth was capitalized.

He looked quickly at her and she sensed the unspoken, unguarded question that flicked across his mind.

"No," she told him, "not religion. Just Truth. The plain and simple Truth."

He almost believed her, for there was a quiet conviction in the way she said it, a deep and solid surety.

"The truth of what?" he asked.

"Why, Truth," the old lady said. "Just Truth."

III

It would be, of course, something more than a simple truth. It would have nothing to do with machines, and it would concern neither power nor glory. It would be an inner truth, a mental or a spiritual or a psychological truth that would have a deep and abiding meaning, the sort of truth that men had followed for years and even followed yet in the wish-worlds of their own creation.

The Human lay in the bed close beneath the roof and listened to the night wind that blew itself a lullaby along the eaves and shingles. The house was quiet and the world was quiet except for the singing wind. The world was quiet, and David Grahame could imagine, lying there, how the galaxy would gradually grow quiet under the magic and the spell of what these human-folk had found.

It must be great, he thought, this truth of theirs. It must be powerful and imagination-snaring and all-answering to send them back like this, to separate them from the striving of the galaxy and send them back to this pastoral life of achieved tranquillity in this alien valley, to make them grub the soil for food and cut the trees for warmth, to make them content with the little that they have.

To get along with that little, they must have much of something else, some deep inner conviction, some mystic inner knowledge that has spelled out to them a meaning to their lives, to the mere fact and living of their lives, that no one else can have.

He lay on the bed and pulled the covers up more comfortably about him and hugged himself with inner satisfaction.

Man cowered in one corner of the galactic empire, a maker of gadgets, tolerated only because he was a maker of gadgets and because the other races never could be sure what he might come up with next; so they tolerated him and threw him crumbs enough to keep him friendly but wasted scant courtesy upon him.

Now, finally, Man had something that would win him a place in the respect and the dignity of the galaxy. For a truth is a thing to be respected.

Peace came to him and he would not let it in but fought against it so that he could think, so that he could speculate, imagining first that this must be the truth that the mutant race had found, then abandoning that idea for one that was even better.

Finally the lullabying wind and the sense of peace and the tiredness of his body prevailed against him and he slept.

The last thought that he had was, I must ask them. I must find out.

But it was days before he asked them, for he sensed that they were watching, and he knew that they wondered if he could be trusted with the truth and if he was worthy of it.

He wished to stay; but for politeness' sake he said that he must go and raised no great objection when they said that he must stay. It was as if each one of them knew this was a racial ritual that must be observed, and all were glad, once it was over and done with.

He worked in the fields with Jed and got to know the

neighbors up and down the valley; he sat long evenings talking with Jed and his mother and the daughter and with the other valley folk who dropped in to pass a word or two.

He had expected that they would ask him questions, but they did not; it was almost as if they didn't care, as if they so loved this valley where they lived that they did not even think about the teeming galaxy their far ancestors had left behind to seek here on this world a destiny that was better than common human destiny.

He did not ask them questions, either, for he felt them watching him, and he was afraid that questions would send them fleeing from the strangeness of him.

But he was not a stranger. It took him only a day or two to know that he could be one of them, and so he made himself become one of them and sat for long hours and talked of common gossip that ran up and down the valley, and it was all kindly gossip. He learned many things—that there were other valleys where other people lived, that the silent, deserted village was something they did not fret about, although each of them seemed to know exactly what it was, that they had no ambition and no hope beyond this life of theirs, and all were well content.

He grew content himself, content with the rose-gray morning, with the dignity of labor, with the pride of growing things. But even as he grew content, he knew he could not be content, that he must find the truth they had found and must carry that truth back to the waiting galaxy. Before long a ship would be coming out to explore the village and to study it and before the ship arrived he must know the answer; when the ship arrived he must be standing on the ridge above the village to tell them what he'd found.

One day Jed asked him, "You will be staying with us?"

David shook his head. "I have to go back, Jed. I would like to stay, but I must go back."

Jed spoke slowly, calmly. "You want the Truth? That's it?"

"If you will give it to me," David said.

"It is yours to have," said Jed. "You will not take it back."

That night Jed said to his daughter, "Alice, teach David how to read our writing. It is time he knew."

In the corner by the fireplace the old lady sat rocking in her chair.

"Aye," she said. "It is time he read the Truth."

IV

The key had come by special messenger from its custodian five valleys distant, and now Jed held it in his hand and slid it into the lock of the door in the building that stood in the center of the old, quiet, long-deserted village.

"This is the first time," Jed said, "that the door has been opened except for the ritualistic reading. Each hundred years the door is opened and the Truth is read so that those who are then living may know that it is so."

He turned the key and David heard the click of the tumblers turning in the lock.

"That way," said Jed, "we keep it actual fact. We do not allow it to become a myth.

"It is," he said, "too important a thing to become a myth."

Jed turned the latch and the door swung open just an inch or two.

"I said ritualistic reading," he said, "and perhaps that is not quite right. There is no ritual to it. Three persons are chosen and they come here on the appointed day and each of them reads the Truth and then they go back as living witnesses. There is no more ceremony than there is with you and me."

"It is good of you to do this for me," David said.

"We would do the same for any of our people who should doubt the Truth," said Jed. "We are a very simple people and we do not believe in red tape or rules. All we do is live.

"In just a little while," he said, "you will understand why we are simple people."

He swung the door wide open and stepped to one side so that David might walk in ahead of him. The place was one large room and it was neat and orderly. There was some dust, but not very much.

Half the room was filled to three quarters of its height with a machine that gleamed in the dull light that came from some source high in the roof.

"This is our machine," said Jed.

And so it was gadgetry, after all. It was another machine, perhaps a cleverer and sleeker machine, but it was still a gadget and the human race were still gadgeteers.

"Doubtless you wondered why you found no machines," said Jed. "The answer is that there is only one, and this is it."

"Just one machine!"

"It is an answerer," said Jed. "A logic. With this machine, there is no need of any others."

"You mean it answers questions?"

"It did at one time," said Jed. "I presume it still would if there were any of us who knew how to operate it. But there is no need of asking further questions."

"You can depend on it?" asked David. "That is, you can be sure that it tells the truth?"

"My son," Jed said soberly, "our ancestors spent thousands of years making sure that it would tell the truth. They did nothing else. It was not only the life work of each trained technician, but the life work of the race. And when they were sure that it would know and tell the truth, when they were certain that there could be no slightest error in the logic of its calculations, they asked two questions of it."

"Two questions?"

"Two questions," Jed said. "And they found the Truth."

"And the Truth?"

"The Truth," Jed said, "is here for you to read. Just as it came out those centuries ago."

He led the way to a table that stood in front of one panel of the great machine. There were two tapes upon the table, lying side by side. The tapes were covered by some sort of transparent preservative.

"The first question," said Jed, "was this: 'What is the purpose of the universe?' Now read the top tape, for that is the answer."

David bent above the table and the answer was upon the tape:

The universe has no purpose. The universe just happened.

"And the second question . . ." said Jed, but there was no need for him to finish, for what the question had been was implicit in the wording of the second tape:

112

Life has no significance. Life is an accident.

"And that," said Jed, "is the Truth we found. That is why we are a simple people."

David lifted stricken eyes and looked at Jed, the descendant of that mutant race that was to have brought power and glory, respect and dignity, to the gadgeteering humans.

"I am sorry, son," said Jed. "That is all there is."

They walked out of the room, and Jed locked the door and put the key into his pocket.

"They'll be coming soon," said Jed, "the ones who will be sent out to explore the village. I suppose you will be waiting for them?"

David shook his head. "Let's go back home," he said.

RETROGRADE EVOLUTION

THE trader had saved some space in the cargo hold for the babu root which, ounce for ounce, represented a better profit than all the other stuff he carried from the dozen planets the ship had visited.

But something had happened to the *Google* villages on the plant Zan. There was no babu root waiting for the ship and the trader had raged up and down, calling forth upon all *Googles* dire maledictions combed from a score of languages and cultures.

High in his cubbyhole, one level down from the control room and the captain's quarters, Steve Sheldon, the space ship's assigned co-ordinator, went through reel after reel of records pertaining to the planet and studied once again the bible of his trade, Dennison's *Key to Sentient Races*. He searched for a hidden clue, clawing through his close-packed memory for some forgotten fact which might apply.

But the records were very little help.

Zan, one of the planets by-passed on the first wave of exploration, had been discovered five centuries before. Since that time traders had made regular visits there to pick up babu root. In due time the traders had reported it to Culture. But Culture, being busy with more important things than a backwoods planet, had done no more than file the report for future action and then, of course, had forgotten all about it.

No survey, therefore, had ever been made of Zan, and the record reels held little more than copies of trading contracts, trading licenses, applications for monopolies and hundreds of sales invoices covering the five hundred years of trade. Interspersed here and there were letters and reports on the culture of the *Googles* and descriptions of the planet, but since the reports were by obscure planet-hoppers and not by trained observers they were of little value.

Sheldon found one fairly learned dissertation upon the babu root. From that paper he learned that the plant grew nowhere else but on Zan and was valuable as the only known cure for a certain disease peculiar to a certain sector of the galaxy. At first the plant had grown wild and had been gathered by the *Googles* as an article of commerce, but in more recent years, the article said, some attempts had been made to cultivate it since the wild supply was waning.

Sheldon could pronounce neither the root's drug derivative nor the disease it cured, but he shrugged that off as of no consequence.

Dennison devoted less than a dozen lines to Zan and from them Sheldon learned no more than he already knew: *Googles* were humanoid, after a fashion, and with Type 10 culture, varying from Type 10-A to Type 10-H; they were a peaceful race and led a pastoral existence; there were thirty-seven known tribal villages, one of which exercised benevolent dictatorship over the other thirty-six. The top-dog village, however, changed from time to time, apparently according to some peaceful rotational system based upon a weird brand of politics. *Googles* were gentle people and did not resort to war.

And that was all the information there was. It wasn't much to go on.

But, for that matter, Sheldon comforted himself, no co-ordinator ever had much to go on when his ship ran into a snag. A co-ordinator did not actually begin to function constructively until everyone, including himself, was firmly behind the eight-ball.

Figuring the way out from behind the eight-ball was a co-ordinator's job. Until he faced dilemma, a yard wide and of purest flecce, he was hardly needed. There was, of course, the matter of riding herd on traders to see that they didn't cheat, beyond a reasonable limit, the aliens with whom they traded, of seeing that they violated no alien tabus and outraged no alien ethics, that they abided by certain restraints and observed minimum protocol, but that was routine policing —just ordinary chores.

Now, after an uneventful cruise, something had finally happened—there was no babu root and Master Dan Hart of the starship *Emma* was storming around and raising hell and getting nowhere fast.

Sheldon heard him now, charging up the stairs to the co-ordinator's cubbyhole. Judging the man's temper by the tumult of his progress, Sheldon swept the reels to one side of the desk and sat back in his chair, settling his mind into that unruffled calm which went with his calling.

"Good day to you, Master Hart," said Sheldon when the irate skipper finally entered.

"Good day to you, Co-ordinator," said Hart, although obviously, it pained him to be civil.

"I've been looking through the records," Sheldon told him. "There's not much to go on."

"You mean," said Hart, with rage seething near the surface, "that you've no idea of what is going on."

"Not the slightest," said Sheldon cheerfully.

"It's got to be better than that," Hart told him. "It's got to be a good deal better than that, Mister Co-ordinator. This is one time you're going to earn your pay. I carry you for years at a good stiff salary, not because I want to, but because Culture says I have to, and during all that time there's nothing, or almost nothing, for you to do. But now there *is* something for you to do. Finally there *is* something to make you earn your pay. I've put up with you, had you in my hair, stumbled over you, and I've held my tongue and temper, but now that there's a job to do, I'm going to see you do it."

He thrust out his head like an angry turtle. "You understand that, don't you, Mister Co-ordinator?"

"I understand," said Sheldon.

115

"You're going to get to work on it," said Hart. "You'll get on it right away."

"I'm working on it now."

"Indeed," said Mister Hart.

"I've satisfied myself," said Sheldon, "that there's nothing in the records."

"And what do you do now?"

"Observe and think," said Sheldon.

"Observe and think!" yelped Hart, stricken to the core.

"Maybe try a hunch or two," said Sheldon. "Eventually we'll find out what's the trouble."

"How long?" asked Hart. "How long will all this mummery take?"

"That's something I can't tell you."

"So you can't tell me that. I must remind you, Mister Co-ordinator, that time spells money in the trading business."

"You're ahead of schedule," Sheldon told him calmly. "You've shaved everything on the entire cruise. You were brusque in your trading almost to the point of rudeness despite the standards of protocol that Culture has set up. I was forced time after time to impress upon you the importance of that protocol. There were other times when I let you get away with murder. You've driven the crew in violation of Labor's program of fair employment. You've acted as if the devil were only a lap behind you. Your crew will get a needed rest while we untangle this affair. The loss of time won't harm you."

Hart took it because he didn't know quite how far he could push the quiet man who sat behind the desk. He shifted his tactics.

"I have a contract for the babu," he said, "and the license for this trade route. I don't mind telling you I'd counted on the babu. If you don't shake loose that babu, I'll sue . . ."

"Don't be silly," Sheldon said.

"They were all right five years ago," said Hart, "the last trip we were here. A culture just can't go to pot in that length of time."

"What we have here," said Sheldon, "is something more complicated than mere going to pot. Here we have some scheme, some plan, something deliberate.

"The Type 10 culture village stands there to the west

116

of us, just a mile or two away, deserted, with its houses carefully locked and boarded up. Everything all tidy, as if its inhabitants had moved away for a short time and meant to come back in the not too distant future. And a mile or two outside that Type 10 village we have instead another village and a people that average Type 14."

"It's crazy," Hart declared. "How could a people lose four full culture points? And even if they did, why would they move from a Type 10 village to a collection of reed huts? Even barbarian conquerors who capture a great city squat down and camp in the palaces and temples—no more reed huts for them."

"I don't know," said Sheldon. "It's my job to find out."

"And how to correct it?"

"I don't know that, either. It may take centuries to correct."

"What gets me," said Hart, "is that god-house. And the greenhouse behind it. There's babu growing in that greenhouse."

"How do you know it's babu?" Sheldon demanded. "All you've ever seen of babu was the root."

"Years ago," said Hart, "one of the natives took me out and showed me. I'll never forget it. There was a patch of it that seemed to cover acres. There was a fortune there. But I couldn't pull up a single plant. They were saving it, they said, until the root grew bigger."

"I've told the men," said Sheldon, "to keep clear of that god-house and now, Hart, I'm telling you. And that means the greenhouse, too. If I catch anyone trying to get at babu root or anything else growing in that greenhouse, there'll be hell to pay."

A short time after Hart left, the chief of the *Google* village climbed the stairs to call on the co-ordinator.

He was a filthy character, generously inhabited by vermin. He didn't know what chairs were for and squatted on the floor. So Sheldon left his chair and squatted down to face him, but immediately shuffled back a step or two, for the chief was rather high.

Sheldon spoke in *Google* lingo haltingly, for it was the first time he had used it since co-ordinator college days. There is, he supposed, not a man on the ship that could not speak it better than I, for each of the crew was on Zan before and this is my first trip.

"The chief is welcome," Sheldon said.

"Favor?" asked the chief.

"Sure, a favor," Sheldon said.

"Dirty stories," said the chief. "You know some dirty stories?"

"One or two," said Sheldon. "But I'm afraid they're not too good."

"Tell 'em," said the chief, busily scratching himself with one hand. With the other he just as busily picked mud from between his toes.

So Sheldon told him the one about the woman and the twelve men marooned on an asteroid.

"Huh?" said the chief.

So Sheldon told him another one, much simpler and more directly obscene.

"That one all right," said the chief, not laughing. "You know another one?"

"That's all I know," said Sheldon, seeing no point in going on. "Now you tell me one," he added, for he figured that one should do whatever possible to get along with the aliens, especially when it was his job to find what made them tick.

"I not know any," said the chief. "Maybe someone else?"

"Greasy Ferris," Sheldon told him. "He's the cook, and he's got some that will curl your hair."

"So good," said the chief, getting up to go.

At the door he turned. "You remember another one," he said, "you be sure to tell me."

Sheldon could see, without half trying, that the chief was serious about his stories.

Sheldon went back to his desk, listening to the soft paddling of the chief's feet going down the catwalk. The communicator chirped. It was Hart.

"The first of the scout boats are in," he said. "They reported on five other villages and they are just the same as this. The *Googles* have deserted their old villages and are living in filthy huts just a mile or two away. And every one of those reed-hut villages has a god-house and a greenhouse."

"Let me know as soon as the other boats come in," said Sheldon, "although I don't suppose we can hope for much. The reports probably will be the same."

"Another thing," said Hart. "The chief asked us to come down to the village for a pow-wow tonight. I told him that we'd come."

"That's some improvement," Sheldon said. "For the first few days they didn't notice us. Either didn't notice us or ran away."

"Any ideas yet, Mister Co-ordinator?"

"One or two."

"Doing anything about them?"

"Not yet," said Sheldon. "We have lots of time."

He clicked off the squawk box and sat back. Ideas? Well, one maybe. And not a very good one.

A purification rite? An alien equivalent of a return to nature? It didn't click too well. For, with a Type 10 culture, the *Googles* never strayed far enough from nature to want to return to it.

Take a Type 10 culture. Very simple, of course, but fairly comfortable. Not quite on the verge of the machine age, but almost—yes, just short of the machine age. A sort of golden age of barbarism. Good substantial villages with a simple commerce and sound basic economics. Peaceful dictatorship and pastoral existence. Not too many laws to stumble over. A watered-down religion without an excess of tabus. One big happy family with no sharp class distinction.

And they had deserted that idyllic life.

Crazy? Of course it was crazy.

As it stands now the *Googles* seem barely to get along. Their vocabulary is limited; why, I speak the language even better than the chief, Sheldon told himself.

Their livelihood was barely above the survival level. They hunted and fished, picked some fruit and dug some roots, and went a little hungry—and all the time the garden patches outside the deserted villages lay fallow, waiting for the plow and hoe, waiting for the seed, but with evidence of having been worked only a year or so before. And in those patches undoubtedly they had grown the babu plants as well as vegetables. But the *Googles* now apparently knew nothing of plow or hoe or seed. Their huts were ill-made and dirty. There was family life, but on a moral level that almost turned one's stomach. Their weapons were of stone and they had no agricultural implements.

Retrogression? No, not just simple retrogression. For even in the retrogression, there was paradox.

In the center of the Type 14 village to which the *Googles* had retreated stood the god-house, and back of the god-house stood the greenhouse with babu growing in it. The greenhouse was built of glass and nowhere else in the Type 14 village was there any sign of glass. No Type 14 alien could have built that greenhouse, nor the god-house, either. No mere hut, that god-house, but a building made of quarried stone and squared timbers, with its door locked tight by some ingenious means that no one yet had figured out. Although, to tell the truth, no one had spent much time on it. On an alien planet, visitors don't monkey with a god-house.

I swear, said Sheldon, talking aloud to himself, that the god-house was never built by that gang out there. It was built, if I don't miss my guess, before the retrogression. And the greenhouse, too.

On Earth when we go away for a vacation and have potted flowers or plants that we wish to keep alive, we take them to a neighbor or a friend to care for them, or make arrangements for someone to come in and water them.

And when we go on vacation from a Type 10 culture back to Type 14, and we have some babu plants that are valuable as seed stock, what do we do with them? We can't take them to a neighbor, for our neighbor, too, is going on vacation. So we do the best we can. We build a greenhouse and rig it up with a lot of automatic gadgets that will take care of the plants until we come back to care for them ourselves.

And that meant, that almost proved, that the retrogression was no accident.

The crew slicked themselves up for the pow-wow, putting on clean clothes, taking baths and shaving. Greasy hauled out his squeeze box and tried a tune or two by way of warming up. A gang of would-be singers in the engine room practiced close harmony, filling the ship with their caterwauling. Master Hart caught one of the tubemen with a bottle that had been smuggled aboard. He broke the man's jaw with one well-directed lick, a display of enthusiastic discipline which Sheldon told Hart was just a bit extreme.

Sheldon put on a semidress outfit, feeling slightly silly at dressing up for a tribe of savages, but he salved his conscience with the feeling that, after all, he was not going all the way with a full-dress uniform.

He was putting on his coat when he heard Hart come down from his quarters and turn toward his cubbyhole.

"The rest of the scouts came in," said Hart from the door.

"Well?"

"They are all the same. Every single tribe has moved out of its old village and set up a bunch of hovels built around a higher culture god-house and a greenhouse. They're dirty and half starving, just like this bunch out here."

"I suspected it," said Sheldon.

Hart squinted at him, as if he might be calculating where he best could hang one.

"It's logical," said Sheldon. "Certainly you see it. If one village went native for a certain reason, so would all the rest."

"The reason, Mister Co-ordinator, is what I want to know."

Sheldon said calmly, "I intend to discover it."

And he thought: It was for a reason, then. If all of them went native, it was for some purpose, according to some plan! And to work out and co-ordinate such a plan among thirty-seven villages would call for smooth-working communication, far better than one would look for in a Type 10 culture.

Feet pounded on the catwalk, thundering up. Hart swung around to face the door, and Greasy, charging into it, almost collided with him.

The cook's eyes were round with excitement and he was puffing with his run.

"They're opening the god-house," he gasped. "They just got the—"

"I'll have their hides for this," Hart bellowed. "I issued orders not to fool around with it."

"It isn't the men, sir," said Greasy. "It's the *Googles*. They've opened up their god-house."

Hart swung around to Sheldon.

121

"We can't go," he said.

"We have to go," Sheldon said. "They've invited us. At this particular moment, we can't offend them."

"Side-arms, then," said Hart.

"With orders not to use them except as a last resort."

Hart nodded. "And some men stationed up here with rifles to cover us if we have to run for it."

"That sounds sensible," said Sheldon.

Hart left at the double.

Greasy turned to go.

"Just a moment, Greasy. You saw the god-house standing open?"

"That I did, sir."

"And what were you doing down there?"

"Why, sir . . ." From his face, Sheldon could see that Greasy was fixing up a lie.

"I told him one," said Sheldon. "He didn't seem to get it."

The cook grinned. "Well, you see, it was like this. Some of them *Googles* were cooking up some brew and I gave them some points, just to help along a bit. They were doing it all wrong, sir, and it seemed a pity to have their drinking spoiled by ignorance. So . . ."

"So, tonight you went down to get your cut."

"That, sir, was about the way it was."

"I see," said Sheldon. "Tell me, Greasy, have you been giving them some pointers on other things as well?"

"Well, I told the chief some stories."

"Did he like them?"

"I don't know," said Greasy. "He didn't laugh, but he seemed to like them all right."

"I told him one," said Sheldon. "He didn't seem to get it."

"That might be the case," said Greasy. "If you'll pardon me, sir, a lot of your stories are a bit too subtle."

"That's what I thought," said Sheldon. "Anything else?"

"Anything—oh, I see. Well, there was one fixing up a reed to make a flute and he was doing it all wrong . . ."

"So you showed him how to make a better flute?"

"That I did," said Greasy.

"I am sure," said Sheldon, "that you feel you've put in some powerful licks for progress, helping along a very backward race."

"Huh," said Greasy.

"That's all right," said Sheldon. "If I were you, I'd go easy on that brew."

"That's all you want of me?" asked Greasy, already halfway out the door.

"That's all I want," said Sheldon. "Thanks, Greasy."

A better brew, thought Sheldon. A better brew and a better flute and a string of dirty stories.

He shook his head. None of it, as yet, added up to anything.

Sheldon squatted on one side of the chief and Hart squatted on the other. Something about the chief had changed. For one thing, he was clean. He no longer scratched and he was no longer high. There was no mud between his toes. He had trimmed both his beard and hair, scraggly as they were, and had combed them out—a vast improvement over the burrs and twigs and maybe even birds' nests once lodged in them.

But there was something more than cleanliness. Sheldon puzzled over it even as he tried to force himself to attack the dish of food that had been placed in front of him. It was a terrible-looking mess and the whiff he had of it wasn't too encouraging, and, to make matters worse, there were no forks.

Beside him, the chief slurped and gurgled, shoveling food into his mouth with a swift, two-handed technique. Listening to his slurping, Sheldon realized what else was different about him. The chief spoke better now. Just that afternoon he had talked a pidgin version of his own tongue, and now he talked with a command of the language that amounted almost to fluency!

Sheldon shot a glance around the circle of men squatted on the ground. Each Earthman was seated with a *Google* to each side of him, and between the slurping and the slopping, the natives made a point of talking to the Earthmen. Just like the Chamber of Commerce boys do when they have guests, thought Sheldon—doing their best to make their guests content and happy and very much at home. And that was a considerable contrast with the situation when the ship first had landed, when the natives had peeked out of doorways or had merely grunted, when they'd not actually run away.

123

The chief polished his bowl with circling fingers, then sucked his fingers clean with little moans of delight. Then he turned to Hart and said, "I observe that in the ship you eat off an elevated structure. I have puzzled over that."

"A table," mumbled Hart, having hard going with his fingers.

"I do not understand," said the chief, and Hart went on to tell him what a table was and its advantage over squatting on the ground.

Sheldon, seeing that everyone else was eating, although with something less than relish, dipped his fingers in the bowl. Mustn't gag, he told himself. No matter how bad it is, I mustn't gag.

But it was even worse than he had imagined and he did gag. But no one seemed to notice.

After what seemed interminable hours of gastronomical torture, the meal was done, and during that time Sheldon told the chief about knives and forks and spoons, about cups, about chairs, pockets in trousers and coats, clocks and watches, the theory of medicine, the basics of astronomy, and the quaint Earthian custom of hanging paintings on a wall. Hart told him about the principles of the wheel and the lever, the rotation of crops, sawmills, the postal system, bottles for the containment of liquid and the dressing of building stone.

Just encyclopedias, thought Sheldon. My God, the questions that he asks. Just encyclopedias for a squatting, slurping savage of a Type 14 culture. Although, wait a minute now—was it still 14? Might it not, within the last half day, have risen to a Type 13? Washed, combed, trimmed, with better social graces and a better language —it's crazy, he told himself. Utterly and absolutely insane to think that such a change could take place in the span of half a day.

From where he sat he could look across the circle directly at the god-house with its open door. And staring at the black maw of the doorway, in which there was no hint of life or light, he wondered what was there and what might come out of it—or go into it. For he was certain that within the doorway lay the key to the enigma of the *Googles* and their retrogression, since it seemed

124

that the god-house itself must have been erected in preparation for the retrogression. *No Type 14 culture,* he decided, *could have erected it.*

After the meal was over, the chief rose and made a short speech, telling them that he was glad the visitors could eat with the tribe that night, and that now they would have some entertainment. Then Hart stood up and made a speech, saying they were glad to be on Zan and that his men had come prepared to offer a small matter of entertainment in return, if the chief would care to see it. The chief said he and his people would. Then he clapped his hands as a signal and about a dozen *Google* girls came out and marched around in the center of the circle, going through a ritual figure, weaving and dancing without benefit of music. Sheldon saw that the *Googles* watched intently, but none of it made much sense to him, well-grounded as he was in alien ritual habits.

Finally it was over. One or two misguided Earthmen clapped, but quickly subsided into embarrassed silence when everyone else sat in deathly quiet.

Then a *Google* with a reed pipe—perhaps the very one, Sheldon thought, upon which Greasy had done his consultative engineering—squatted in the center of the circle and piped away with a weird inconsistency that would have put to shame even the squeakiest of Earthly bagpipers. It lasted for a long time and seemed to get nowhere, but this time the ship's crew, perhaps in relief at the ending, finally, of the number, whooped and clapped and yelled and whistled as if for an encore, although Sheldon was fairly sure they meant quite the opposite.

The chief turned to Sheldon and asked what the men were doing. Sheldon had a reasonably hard time explaining to him the custom of applause.

The two numbers, it turned out, were the sum total of the entertainment program whomped by the *Googles,* and Sheldon would have liked to ask the chief if that was all the village could muster, a fact which he suspected, but he refrained from inquiring.

The ship's crew took over, then.

The engine-room gang gathered together, with their arms around each other's shoulders in the best barber-shop tradition and sang half a dozen songs, with Greasy laboring away on the squeeze box to accompany them. They sang old songs of Earth, the songs all spacemen sing, with unshed tears brightening their eyes.

It wasn't long before others of the crew joined in, and in less than an hour the ship's entire complement was howling out the songs, beating the ground with the flats of their hands to keep time and flinging back their heads to yelp the Earth words into the alien sky.

Then someone suggested they should dance. One of the tubemen called the sets while Greasy humped lower over his squeeze box, pumping out "Old Dan Tucker" and "Little Brown Jug" and "The Old Gray Mare" and others of their kind.

Just how it happened Sheldon didn't see, but all at once there were more sets. The *Googles* were dancing, too, making a few mistakes, but their Earthmen teachers guided them through their paces until they got the hang of it.

More and more of them joined in, and finally the entire village was dancing, even the chief, while Greasy pumped away, with the sweat streaming down his face. The *Google* with the reed pipe came over after a while and sat down beside Greasy. He seemed to have got the technique of how to make the music too, for his piping notes came out loud and clear, and he and Greasy hunkered there, playing away like mad while all the others danced. The dancers yelled and hollered and stamped the ground and turned cartwheels which were totally uncalled for and strictly out of place. But no one seemed to care.

Sheldon found himself beside the god-house. He and Hart were alone, pushed outward by the expanding dance space.

Said Hart: "Mister Co-ordinator, isn't that the damnedest thing that you have ever seen."

Sheldon agreed. "One thing you have to say about it: The party is a wingding."

Greasy brought the news in the morning when Sheldon was having breakfast in his cubbyhole.

"They've dragged something out of that there god-house," Greasy said.

"What is it, Greasy?"

126

"I wouldn't know," said Greasy. "And I didn't want to ask."

"No," said Sheldon, gravely. "No, I can appreciate you wouldn't."

"It's a cube," said Greasy. "A sort of latticework affair and it's got shelves, like, in it, and it don't make no sense at all. It looks something like them pictures you showed me in the book one time."

"Diagrams of atomic structure?"

"That's exactly it," said Greasy. "Except more complicated."

"What are they doing with it?"

"Just putting it together. And puttering around with it. I couldn't tell exactly *what* they were doing with it."

Sheldon mopped up his plate and shoved it to one side. He got up and shrugged into his coat. "Let's go down and see," he said.

There was quite a crowd of natives around the contraption when they arrived, and Sheldon and Greasy stood on the outskirts of the crowd, keeping quiet and saying nothing, being careful not to get in the way.

The cube was made of rods of some sort and was about twelve feet on each side, and the rods were joined together with a peculiar disc arrangement. The whole contraption looked like something a kid with a full-blown imagination might dream up with a super-tinker-toy set.

Within the cube itself were planes of glasslike material, and these, Sheldon noticed, were set with almost mathematical precision, great attention having been paid to the exact relationship between the planes.

As they watched, a heavy box was brought out of the god-house by a gang of *Googles,* who puffed and panted as they lugged it to the cube. They opened the box and took out several objects, carved of different materials, some wood, some stone, others of unfamiliar stuff. These they set in what appeared to be prescribed positions upon the various planes.

"Chess," said Greasy.

"What?"

"Chess," said Greasy. "It looks like they're setting up a game of chess."

"Could be," said Sheldon, thinking, if it is a chess

game, it is the wildest, most fantastic, toughest game I have ever seen.

"They got some screwy chess games, now," said Greasy. "Fairy chess, they call it, with more squares to the board and more pieces, different than the ones you use just regular. Me, I never could rightly get the hang of even normal chess."

The chief saw them and came over.

"We are very confident," he said. "With the help you gave us, we can't help but win."

"That is gratifying," Sheldon said.

"These other villages," said the chief, "haven't got a ghost. We have them pegged dead center. This will be three times, hand-running."

"You are to be congratulated," said Sheldon, wondering what it was all about.

"It's been a long time," said the chief.

"So it has," said Sheldon, still very much at sea.

"I must go now," said the chief. "We start now."

"Wait a second," Sheldon asked him. "You are playing a game?"

"You might call it that," the chief admitted.

"With these other villages—all the other villages?"

"That's right," said the chief.

"How long does it take? With all those villages, you and the other thirty-six . . ."

"This one won't take long," the chief declared, with a knowing leer.

"Good luck, chief," said Sheldon and watched him walk away.

"What's going on?" asked Greasy.

"Let's get out of here," said Sheldon. "I have work to do."

Hart hit the ceiling when he learned the kind of work that Sheldon had to do.

"You can't third-degree my men!" he shouted. "I won't have it. They haven't done a thing."

"Master Hart," said Sheldon, "you will have the men line up. I'll see them in my quarters, one at a time, and I won't third-degree them. I just want to talk to them."

"Mister Co-ordinator," said Hart, "I'll do the talking for them."

"You and I, Master Hart," said Sheldon, "did our talking last night. Much too much of it."

For hours on end, Sheldon sat in his cubbyhole which the men filed in one at a time and answered the questions that he shot at them:

"What questions did the *Googles* ask you?"

"How did you answer them?"

"Did they seem to understand?"

Man by man the notes piled up, and at last the job was done.

Sheldon locked the door, took a bottle from his desk and had a liberal snort; then he put the bottle back again and settled down to work, going through the notes.

The communicator beeped at him.

"The scouts are in," said Hart's voice, "and every single village has one of those cubes set up in front of their godhouse. They're sitting around in a circle and they seem to be playing some sort of game. Every once in a while someone gets up from the circle and makes a move on one of the planes in the cube and then goes back and sits down again."

"Anything else?"

"Nothing else," said Hart. "That was what you wanted, wasn't it?"

"Yes," said Sheldon, "I guess that was what I wanted."

"Tell me one thing," asked Hart. "Who are they playing?"

"They're playing one another."

"One another what?"

"The villages," said Sheldon. "The villages are playing against one another."

"You mean thirty-seven villages?"

"That's what I mean."

"Would you tell me just how in hell thirty-seven villages can play one single game?"

"No, I can't," said Sheldon. But he had the terrible feeling that he could. That he could make a guess at least.

When it had become apparent that the retrogression was a planned affair, he remembered, he had wondered about the problem of communications which would have been necessary to have thirty-seven villages simultaneously retrogress. It would have taken, he had told himself, a higher order of communications than one would expect to find in a Type 10 culture.

And here it was again—an even tougher communications job, an odd, round-robin game in which these same thirty-seven villages played a game upon a complicated board.

There is one answer for it, he told himself. It simply couldn't be, but there is no other answer for it—telepathy —and that is almost unthinkable in a Type 10 culture, let alone a Type 14.

He clicked off the squawk box and went back to work. He took a large sheet of paper to serve as a master chart and thumbtacked it to the desk, then started on the notes, beginning with the top one and going through to the very last. And when he had finished the chart, he sat back and looked at it, then put in a call for Hart.

Five minutes later Hart climbed the stairs and knocked at the door. Sheldon unlocked it and let him in. "Sit down, Hart," he said.

"You have something?"

"I think I have," said Sheldon. He gestured at the sheet thumbtacked on the desk. "It's all there."

Hart stared at the chart. "I don't see a thing."

"Last night," said Sheldon, "we went to the *Google* pow-wow, and in the short time we spent there, we gave that particular village the most complete and comprehensive outline of a Type 10 culture that you have ever seen. But what really scares me is that we went somewhere *beyond* Type 10. I haven't worked it out completely, but it looks nearer Type 9M than Type 10."

"We what?"

"They pumped it out of us," said Sheldon. "Each of our men was questioned about certain cultural matters, and in not a single instance was there duplication. Each of the set of questions asked was a different set of questions. Just as if those *Googles* were assigned certain questions."

"What does it mean?" asked Hart.

"It means," said Sheldon, "that we have interfered in one of the slickest social setups in the entire galaxy. I hope to God . . ."

"Slick social setup! You mean the *Googles?*"

"I mean the *Googles,*" Sheldon said.

"But they never amounted to anything," Hart said. "They never will amount to anything. They . . ."

"Think hard," said Sheldon, "and try to tell me what is the most outstanding thing about the *Google* culture. We have a history of five hundred years of trade with them. During those five hundred years there is one fact about them that sticks up like a bandaged thumb."

"They're dumb," said Hart.

"Not from here, they aren't."

"They never got anywhere," said Hart. "Weren't even going anywhere, far as I could see."

"That's part of it," said Sheldon. "Static culture."

"I'll be damned," said Hart, "if I'll play guessing games with you. If you have something on your mind . . ."

"I have *peace* on the mind," said Sheldon. "In all the five hundred years we've known the *Googles,* there has been no dissension among them. They've never fought a war. That is something that cannot be said for any other planet."

"They are just too dumb to fight," said Hart.

"Too *smart* to fight," said Sheldon. "*The Googles,* Master Hart, have done something no other people, no other culture, has ever been able to do in all galactic history. They've found a way in which to outlaw war!"

For thousands upon thousands of years, empire after empire had been built among the stars and upon the many planets that circled round the stars.

And one by one, lonely and beaten, each empire had fallen, and one by one other empires had risen to take their place and in their turn had fallen. And those that existed in this day would fall in time.

This is the old, old cycle, Sheldon told himself, the ancient disease of force and arrogance and desperation —the ageless pattern of cultural development.

Never had a day existed since the first beginning that there had not been war at one place or another within the galaxy.

War came about because of economic pressure, mostly, although there were other causes—the ambitions of a certain being or of a certain race, the strange death-wish psychology which bloomed in certain cultures, an overweening racism, or a religion that spoke in terms of blood and death, rather than in terms of love and life.

Break down the causes of war, Sheldon thought, and we would find a pattern—certain factors which made for war and certain other factors which made for victory, once war had been invoked.

Now, suppose we made a study of war, its causes and the winning of it. Suppose we worked out the relevant relationships which each factor held to all the other factors, and not only that, but the relevant power of certain groups of factors against other groups of factors—factors of racial ingenuity and technology, of the human spirit, of logistics, of cultural development and the urge to protect and retain that culture, and hatred or the capacity to hate, all the many factors, tangible and intangible, which went into the making and the winning of a war.

And broken down into concrete terms, what would some of those factors be? What factors pushed a culture to the point of war? What factors made a victor? Certainly not just steel and firepower, certainly not courage alone, or generalship alone, or logistics or any other thing that could stand alone.

There would be other things as well, little, inconsequential, homely items, like sitting in a chair instead of squatting on the floor to eat, or using a knife and fork and not fingers. And other things, like dirty stories and better-drinking likker and a better pipe fashioned from a reed. For into all of these would go certain principles —the principle involved in the making of a better beer might light the way to manufacture a chemical that could be used in war; the perverted wit that shaped a dirty story might be turned to more destructive use in the propaganda section; the knowledge that made a better musical instrument might be extended to fashion an instrument that was not musical, but deadly.

It would be abilities such as these which would supply the economic pressure that might start a war, or contribute to that sense of superiority and intolerance and invincibility which might incline a tribe to war.

And if we watched the factors which represented these and other abilities, we would know when a war was about to pop.

And it was these same basic abilities and attitudes,

132

plus a million other factors, which would determine who would win if a war should start.

Knowing this, we could assign certain actual values to all these cultural factors, although the value, as in a hand of cards, would be increased or decreased as they occurred in combination.

Sheldon got up and paced the tiny room, three steps up and three steps back.

Suppose then, he thought, we made a game of it—a game of war, with all the factors represented by game pieces assigned sliding values. Suppose we played a game instead of fighting a war. Suppose we let the game decide which side would have won if there had been a war.

Suppose, furthermore, that we watched cultures and detected the rise of those factors which finally lead to war. Suppose we could say that if the rise of certain factors should continue, war would then be inevitable in five years or ten.

Suppose we could do this—then we could catch a war before it started. We could see the danger signals and we would know the crisis point. And when we reached the crisis point, we played a game—we did not fight a war.

Except, Sheldon told himself, it wouldn't work.

We could play a game and decide a war, and once it had been decided, the factors that made for war would still be there; the crisis point would stand. We would be right back where we started; we would not have gained a thing. For the game, while it might decide who would have won the war, would not upset or correct the economic pressure, would not erase the crisis point.

No doubt the game could show which side would have won. It could predict, with a small percentage error, the outcome of a war. But it could not wipe out excess populations, it could not wrest trade advantages from the opposing side—it wouldn't do the job.

It wouldn't work, he told himself. It was a beautiful theory, a great idea, but it just wouldn't work.

We'd have to do more than play a game. We'd have to do a great deal more than play a game.

Besides determining who would have won the war if there had been a war, we would have to remove voluntarily the factors which had brought about the war—

the solid, substantial facts of economic pressure, of intolerance, of all the other factors which would be involved.

It wasn't only the matter of playing a game, but of paying a price as well. There would be a price for peace and we'd have to pay the price.

For there would be more than one set of factors.

There would be the set that showed a war was coming. And there would be another set which would show that beyond a certain point the hard-won formula for peace simply wouldn't work.

It would work, perhaps, for a Type 10 culture, but beyond that, the factors involved might get so complicated that the formula would collapse under its own weight. A Type 10 culture might be able to deal with a factor which represented the cornering of the market on a certain food, but they could not deal with a factor which represented the complexity of galactic banking.

The formula might work for a Type 10 culture, but it might not work for Type 9; it might be utterly worthless for Type 8.

So the *Googles* not only played the game, but they paid the price of peace. And the price of peace was to run the other way. They retreated from advancement. They went clear back to 14 and they stayed there for a while, then went forward rather swiftly, but not as far as they were before they retrogressed. They went back voluntarily, and they stayed back, so they wouldn't fight a war.

They went back, not because war was less likely in a Type 14 culture than in a Type 10 culture, but they went back so that the formula, once it had been used, would be effective; they stayed back so that they had some room to advance before they again reached the point beyond which the formula would break down.

But how would they go back? How would they retreat from a 10 to a 14 culture? Retrogress—sure they would retrogress. They would leave their comfortable village and go back and live in squalor and all the time the gameboard and the pieces and the position values they had earned in their Type 10 existence would be safely locked away inside the god-house. There would come the day when they had advanced far enough so they could play the game, and they played it then, according to the rules and with what they had—unless they hit the jackpot, and a spaceship from a higher culture landed in their midst and handed them on a silver platter, as it were, a load of atom bombs to be used in a bow-and-arrow war.

Sheldon sat down at his desk, and held his head in his hands.

How much, he asked himself, *how much more did we give them than they had before?* Have we wrecked the formula? Have we given them so much that this village just outside the ship can bust the formula wide open? How much tolerance would there be? How far could they advance beyond a Type 10 culture and still be within the safety limit?

He got up and paced the floor again.

It's probably all right, he told himself. They've played the game for five hundred years we know of—for how many thousands of years more than that we simply cannot know. They would not willingly break down the formula; they would know the limit. For there must be a deeply ingrained fear of war within their very culture, or otherwise they would not continue to subscribe to the formula. And it's a simple formula, really. Simple. Like falling off a log! Except—how did a people deliberately retrogress?

Hypnotism? Hypnotism wouldn't work, for what would happen to the hypnotist? He'd remain as a random and dangerous factor.

A clever machine, perhaps, except the *Googles* had no machines at all. So it couldn't be machines.

Drugs, maybe.

There was a root, and out of the root a drug was made to fight a disease peculiar to a certain sector of the galaxy—the babu root. Zan was the only place where the babu plant was grown.

"Good Lord," said Sheldon, "I didn't think of that. I read about it. What was that disease?"

He dug out his reels and put them in the viewer and found the dissertation on the use of the babu root, and he found the name of the disease, which was unpronounceable. He looked through the index of his reels

135

and found a reel with the medical information, and there were few lines on that strange disease:

. . . *nervous disorder, with high emotional tensions involved, in many cases stressing a sense of guilt, arising from the inability to forget past experiences. The drug induces a complete state of forgetfulness, from which the patient gradually recovers, retaining basic precepts rather than the welter of detailed experiences, the impingement of which contributes to his condition.*

That's it, of course! That's the perfect answer!

The *Googles* ate of the babu root, perhaps ceremonially, and they forgot, and in the forgetting they sloughed their culture from them, retrogressing four entire culture points. Then, after a time, the effect of the babu root would gradually wear away and they would remember, and remembering, advance up the cultural scale. They would remember, not the details of their former culture, but only its basic precepts, and in that way they'd not climb as high as they had been before. In that way they'd leave a margin through which they would advance toward the next crisis. Then once again, they'd eat of the babu root and once again war would be averted.

For, while the game would determine who would have won the war if one had been fought, the forgetting and the slow recovery from the babu would wipe out the cause of war, would remove the crisis point.

The formula worked because, even before they played the game, the factors of war would have been upset and the crisis point have already disappeared.

"God forgive us," Sheldon said, "our little grasping souls."

He went back to the desk and sat down. With a hand that suddenly was heavy, he reached out and thumbed up the communicator for a call to Hart.

"What is it now?" rasped Hart.

"Get out of here," Sheldon ordered. "Get off this planet as quickly as you can."

"But the root . . ."

"There isn't any root," said Sheldon. "Not any more, there isn't any root."

"I have a contract."

"Not now," said Sheldon. "It is null and void, contrary to galactic interests."

136

"Contrary!" He could hear Hart choking on his rage. "Look here, Co-ordinator, they need that root out in sector 12. They need . . ."

"They'll synthesize it," Sheldon said. "If they want it they'll have to synthesize it. There is something more important . . ."

"You can't do this," said Hart.

"I can," said Sheldon. "If you think I can't, try me out and see."

He snapped the toggle down and waited, sweating out the issue.

Ten minutes passed before he heard the men running in the ship below, preparing for blast-off.

He watched the planet fade behind them as the ship fled into space.

Courage, he said to himself, thinking of the *Googles,* the bare, cold courage of it. I hope it's not too late. I hope we didn't tempt them too far. I hope they can offset the damage that we did.

There must have been a day when the *Googles* were a great race, building a great civilization—greater, perhaps, than any culture now in the galaxy. For it would have taken a fantastically advanced people to have done what they have done. It was no job for a Type 10 culture, nor for a Type 6 culture, which is the best that Earth itself can boast.

It had taken intelligence and great compassion, sharp analytical ability and sober objectivity to figure out the factors and how they could be used.

And it had taken courage beyond imagination to activate the course those ancient *Googles* had worked out —to trade a culture that might have reached Type 2 or 3, for a Type 10 culture, because their plan for peace would not work beyond a Type 10 culture.

Once having worked, it must now continue working. All the courage of the race must not now be lost. It is a formula that must not be allowed to fail. It must not be allowed to fail because of the profit that traders made out of the babu root. It must not be allowed to fail through contact with other uncouth creatures who might be higher on the cultural yardstick, but who are without the common sense and the courage of the *Googles.*

And another thing—we must not run the chance that the babu root became a mere article of commerce. We could not blind the *Googles* to the greater value of the root, the value in which lay the greatest hope the galaxy had known.

Sheldon went back to the chart he'd made and checked through the information which the *Googles* had pumped out of the crew, and it added up to just slightly more than a Type 10 culture—a Type 9R, perhaps. And that was dangerous, but probably not too much so, for the Type 10A, if the *Googles* ever got that far, probably still represented a certain margin of safety. And there was the matter of the lag in the culture, due to the babu-eating, which would probably add an additional safety margin.

But it had been close. Too close for comfort. It demonstrated another factor, the factor of temptation—and that was something that could not be allowed to continue.

He went back to the record reels and spent hours studying the invoices, and once again he saw the cold, stark courage and the insistent dedication of the *Googles*.

There was not a single item on any of the invoices which went beyond a Type 10 culture.

Imagine, he told himself, *settling for a better hoe when they could have had atomic engines!*

Imagine, for five hundred years, refusing merchandise and comfort that would have made the Googles *a greater people and a happier and more leisured people.*

Greater and happier—and, more than likely, dead.

Once long ago, in mighty cities now hidden in the dust of the planet's surface, the *Googles* must have learned the terrible bitterness of a most artful and accomplished war and must have recoiled from the death and agony and the blind futility, and the knowledge of that day still dwelt within the minds of the *Googles* of today.

And that knowledge the galaxy could not afford to lose.

Sheldon picked up the chart and rolled it into a cylinder and slipped a couple of rubber bands around it. He put the reels away.

For five hundred years the *Googles* had held out against the lure of traders who would have given them anything they asked for the babu root. Traders who, even if they had known the truth, still would have willingly and thoughtlessly wrecked the protective Type 10 culture for the sake of profit.

They had held out for five hundred years. How much longer could they hold out? Not forever, certainly. Perhaps not for a great deal longer.

The chief and his tribe had weakened momentarily in acquiring information beyond the Type 10 culture limit. Might that not mean that already the moral fiber was weakening, that the years of trading had already sown their poison?

And if the *Googles* had not held out—if they did not hold out—the galaxy then would be the poorer and the bloodier.

For the day would come, many years from now perhaps, when it might be safe to make a survey, to conduct a study of this great thing the *Google* had accomplished.

And out of that study certainly would come the first great step toward peace throughout the galaxy, a hint as to how the principle might apply without the stultifying need of a static culture.

But the study itself could not be made for many years. Not until the random factors of the last five hundred years of trade had been swept away.

He sat down at the desk, pulled out the voice-writer, and inserted a sheet of paper.

He spoke a heading which the machine printed quickly:

RECOMMENDATION FOR THE INDEFINITE CLOSING OF THE PLANET ZAN TO ALL VISITORS AND TRADERS.

THE FENCE

HE came down the stairway into the hushed sanctuary of the lounge and stood for a moment to allow his eyes to become accustomed to the perpetual twilight of the place.

A robot waiter went past, tall glasses balanced on the tray.

"Good afternoon, Mr. Craig," he said.

"How are you, Herman?" asked Craig.

"Will you wish something, sir?"

"No, thank you," said Craig. "I'm going out directly."

Herman left. Craig crossed the room and he walked almost on tiptoe. He realized now, for the first time, that he almost always walked on tiptoe here. The only noise that ever was allowed was a cough, and even then it must be a cough that was most discreet. To have spoken to anyone within the confines of the lounge would have been high treason.

The ticker stood in one corner of the room and, in keeping with the place, it was an almost silent ticker. The tape came out and went into a basket, but the basket was well watched and often emptied and the tape never, never spilled out on the carpet.

He picked up the strand of tape and ran it through his fingers, bending low to read the characters, backing through the alphabet until he came to *C* and then he went more slowly.

Cox, 108 1/2; Cotton, 97; Colfield, 92; Cratchfield, 111 1/4; Craig, 75 . . .

Craig, 75!

It had been 78 yesterday and 81 the day before and 83 the day before that. A month ago it had been 96 1/2 and a year ago 120.

He stood with the tape in his hand and looked out over the room. The place seemed, at first glance, to be deserted. But, as he looked, he saw them. There was a bald head peeking over the back of one chair, and over the back of another rose a telltale of smoke from an invisible cigar. There was one who sat facing Craig, but he was so much a part of the chair that at first he seemed invisible. He sat quietly, with his gleaming black shoes and white shirt front and the folded paper held stiffly before him.

Craig turned his head slowly and saw, with a sinking feeling, that there was someone in his chair, just three removed from the right wing of the fireplace. A month ago it would not have happened, a year ago it would have been unthinkable. His personal satisfaction had been high, then.

But they knew that he was slipping. They had seen the tape and talked about it. And they felt contempt for him despite their mealy mouths.

"Poor Craig," they had said to one another. "Such a decent chap. And so young, too."

They would have been consoling.

"He'll come out of it," they'd said. "It's just temporary."

And they had been quite smug about it, no doubt, sure that it was the sort of thing that would never happen to any one of them.

The counselor was kind and helpful, and Craig could see at a glance that he was a man well satisfied and that he liked his work.

"Seventy-five," he said. "That is not good, is it, Mr. Craig?"

"No, it's not," said Craig.

"You are engaged in something?" asked the counselor and he simpered just a little, a professional, polished simper that said he knew that Craig was, of course, but he had to ask.

"Oh," said the counselor. "A most engaging subject. I have known a number of gentlemen who were quite wrapped up in history."

"I specialize," said Craig. "One acre."

"Acre?" asked the counselor, not a little puzzled. "I'm not quite sure . . ."

"The history of one acre," Craig told him. "Trace it back, you know, with a temporal viewer. Hour to hour, day to day. Record in detail, and with appropriate comment and deduction, everything that occurred upon the acre."

"Most novel," said the counselor. "I've never heard of it before."

"You do some screwy things," said Craig.

"Screwy?"

"Well, you strive for effect. You try to be spectacular, but spectacular in a scholarly way, if you understand."

"Yes, I am sure I do," the counselor said, "and yet it seems to me that the study of one acre of the Earth's surface is quite legitimate. There have been others who have limited their studies. There have been histories of

141

families and of cities and of certain rather obscure causes and of the development and evolution of such commonplace things as teapots and coffee cups and antimacassars and such."

"Yes," said Craig, "that is exactly what I thought."

"Tell me, Mr. Craig," asked the counselor, "have you run across anything spectacular on your . . . ah, acre?"

"I have traced the growth of trees," said Craig. "Backwards, you know. From decaying giants to saplings, from saplings to seed. It is quite a trick, this backward tracing. It is a bit confusing, but soon you get used to it. I swear you finally get so that you think in reverse. And then, of course, I have kept a record of birds' nests and and the birds themselves. There's one old lame robin that was quite a character. And flowers, naturally. And the action of the elements on boulders and soil. And weather. I have a fine record of the weather over several thousand years."

"Most interesting," said the counselor.

"There was a murder, too," said Craig, "but it happened just outside the boundary line, so I can't actually include it in the study. The murderer, however, did run across the acre after he committed the deed."

"A murder, Mr. Craig?"

"Exactly," said Craig. "One man killed another, you understand."

"How ghastly," said the counselor.

"I suppose it would be," admitted Craig. "But it was done, you know. The records are filled with murders."

"Anything else?"

"Not yet," said Craig, "although I have some hope. I found some old foundations."

"Buildings?"

"Yes, of buildings. Go back far enough and I'm bound to find the buildings before they went to ruin. That might be interesting. There might be people in them. One of the foundations looked like a residence. Had what appeared to be the footing for a fireplace."

"You might hurry it up a bit," suggested the counselor. "Get there a little faster. People are most interesting."

Craig shook his head. "To make the study valid, I must record in detail. I can't slight the detail to get what's interesting."

The counselor managed to look sorrowful.

"With such an interesting project," he said, "I can't understand why your rating should go down."

"I realized," said Craig, "that no one would care. I would spend years at the study and I would publish my findings and I would give copies to my friends and acquaintances and they would thank me and put the book up on the shelf and never take it down again. I would deposit copies in libraries and you know yourself that no one ever goes to libraries. The only one who would ever read the thing would be myself."

"Surely, Mr. Craig," comforted the counselor, "there are other men who have found themselves in a like position. And they have managed to remain relatively happy and contented."

"That is what I've told myself," said Craig, "but it doesn't work for me."

"We could go into many of the closer aspects of the case," said the counselor, "but I think we should leave that until some future time if it proves necessary. We'll just hit the high points now. Tell me, Mr. Craig, are you fairly well convinced that you cannot continue to be happy with your acre?"

"Yes," said Craig. "I am."

"Not conceding for a moment," said the counselor, with dogged determination, "that your statement to that effect closes our avenue of investigation in that direction, tell me this: Have you considered an alternative?"

"An alternative?"

"Why, certainly. Some other line of work that might prove happier. I have counseled a number of gentlemen who changed their line of work, and it has proved for the best."

"No," said Craig. "I haven't the least idea what I might go into."

"There are a number of openings," said the counselor. "Almost anything you wish. There's snail watching, for example."

"No," said Craig.

"Or stamp collecting," said the counselor. "Or knitting. A lot of gentlemen knit and find it very soothing."

"I don't want to knit," said Craig.

"You could make money."

"What for?" asked Craig.

"Well, now," the counselor said, "that is something I've often wondered, too. There's no need of it, really. All you have to do to get money is go to a bank and ask for some of it. But there are men who actually set out to make money and, if you ask me, they use some rather shady methods. But, be that as it may, they seem to get a great deal of satisfaction doing it."

"What do they do with it once they get it?" asked Craig.

"I wouldn't know," the counselor told him. "One man buried it and then forgot where he buried it and he remained happy the rest of his life running around with a lantern and a shovel looking for it."

"Why the lantern?"

"Oh, I forgot to tell you that. He never hunted it in daylight. He hunted in the night."

"Did he ever find it?"

"Come to think of it," the counselor said, "I don't believe he did."

"I don't think," said Craig, "that I'd care for making money."

"You might join a club."

"I belong to a club," said Craig. "A very fine old club. One of the very finest. Some of the best names and its history runs back to . . ."

"That's not the kind of club I mean," the counselor said. "I mean a group of persons who work for something or who have special interests in common and band themselves together for the better enjoyment of those mutual interests."

"I doubt," said Craig, "that a club would be the answer."

"You might get married," the counselor suggested.

"What? You mean to one woman?"

"That is what I mean."

"And raise a bunch of kids?"

"Many men have done it," said the counselor. "They have been quite satisfied."

"It seems," said Craig, "on the face of it, just a bit obscene."

"There are many other possibilities," the counselor told him. "I can just run through a partial list of them and see if there is anything you might care to think about."

Craig shook his head. "Some other time," he said. "I'll come back again. I want to mull it over."

"You're absolutely sure that you're sour on history?" asked the counselor. "I'd rather steer you back to that than interest you in an alternative."

"I'm sour on it," said Craig. "I shudder when I think of it."

"You could take a vacation," suggested the counselor. "You could freeze your personal satisfaction rating until you returned. Maybe then you could boost it up again."

"I think," said Craig, "that to start with I'll take a little walk."

"A walk," the counselor told him, "is very often helpful."

"What do I owe you?" Craig asked.

"A hundred," the counselor said. "But it's immaterial to me whether you pay or not."

"I know," said Craig. "You work for the love of it."

The man sat on the shore of the little pond and leaned back against a tree. He smoked while he kept an eye on the fishpole stuck into the ground beside him. Close at hand was an unpretentious jug made of earthenware.

He looked up and saw Craig.

"Come on, friend," he said. "Sit down and rest yourself."

Craig came and sat. He pulled out a handkerchief and mopped his brow.

"The sun's a little warm," he said.

"Cool here," said the man. "I fish or loaf around when the sun is high. When the sun goes down I go and hoe my garden."

"Flowers," said Craig. "Now there's an idea. I've often thought it would be fun to raise a garden full of flowers."

"Not flowers," the man said. "Vegetables. I eat them."

"You mean you work to get the things you eat?"

"Uh-huh," said the man. "I spade the ground and rake it to prepare the seed bed. Then I plant the seeds and watch them sprout and grow. I tend the garden and I harvest it. I get enough to eat."

"It must be a lot of work."

"I take it easy," said the man. "I don't let it worry me."

"You could get a robot," Craig told him.

"Yeah, I guess I could. But I don't hold with such contraptions. It would make me nervous."

The cork went under and he made a grab for the pole, but he was too late. The hook came up empty.

"Missed that one," he said placidly. "Miss a lot of them. Don't pay enough attention."

He swung in the hook and baited it with a worm from the can that stood beside him.

"Might have been a turtle," he said. "Turtles are hell on bait."

He swung the tackle out again, stuck the pole back into the ground and settled back against the tree.

"I grew a little extra corn," he said, "and run a batch of moon when my stock is running low. The house ain't much to look at, but it's comfortable. I got a dog and two cats, and I fuss my neighbors."

"Fuss your neighbors?"

"Sure," the man said. "They all think I'm nuts."

He picked up the jug, uncorked it and handed it to Craig. Craig took a drink, prepared for the worst. It wasn't bad at all.

"Took a little extra care with that batch," the man said. "It really pays to do that if you have the time."

"Tell me," said Craig, "are you satisfied?"

"Sure," the man said.

"You must have a nice P.S.," said Craig.

"P.X.?"

"No. P.S. Personal satisfaction rating."

The man shook his head. "I ain't got one of them," he said.

Craig was aghast. "But you have to have!"

"You talk just like that other fellow," said the man. "He was around a while ago. Told me about this P.S. business, but I thought he said P.X. Told me I had to have one. Took it awful hard when I said I wouldn't do it."

"Everyone has a P.S.," said Craig.

"Everyone but me," said the man. "That's what the other fellow said, too. He was some upset about it. Practically read me out of the human race."

He looked sharply at Craig. "Son," he said, "you got troubles on your mind."

Craig nodded.

"Lots of folks have troubles," said the man, "only they don't know it. And you can't start to lick your troubles until you see and recognize them. Things are all upset. No one's living right. There is something wrong."

"My P.S. is way off," said Craig. "I've lost all interest. I know there's something wrong. I can sense it, but I can't put my finger on it."

"They get things given to them," said the man. "They could live the life of Riley and not do a tap of work. They could get food and shelter and clothing and all the luxuries that they want by just asking for them. You want money, so you go to a bank and the bank gives you all you need. You go to a shop and buy a thing and the shopkeeper don't give a tinker's damn if you pay or not. Because, you see, it didn't cost him nothing. He got it given to him. He doesn't have to work for a living. He ain't keeping shop, really. He's just playing at it, like kids would play at keeping store. And there's other people who play at all sorts of other things. They do it to keep from dying of boredom. They don't have to do it. And this P.S. business you talk about is just another play-mechanism, a way of keeping score, a sort of social pressure to keep you on your toes when there is no real reason on all of God's green earth that you should be on your toes. It's meant to keep you happy by giving you something to work for. A high P. S. means high social standing and a satisfied ego. It's clever and ingenious, but it's just playing, too."

Craig stared at the man. "A play world," he said. "You've hit it on the head. That's what it really is."

The man chuckled. "You never thought of it before," he said. "That's the trouble. No one ever thinks. Everyone is so busy trying to convince himself that he's happy and important that he never stops to think. Let me tell you this, son: No man ever is important if he tries to make himself important. It's when he forgets that he's important that he really is important.

"Me," he said. "I have lots of time to think."

"I never thought of it," said Craig, "in just that way before."

"We have no economic worth," the man said. "There's not any of us making our own way. There's not a single one of us worth the energy it would take to kill us.

"Except me," he said. "I raise my own eating and I catch some fish and I snare some rabbits and I make a batch of drinking likker whenever I run out."

"I always thought of our way of life," said Craig, "as the final phase in economic development. That's what they teach the kids. Man has finally achieved economic independence. There is no government and there is no economic fabric. You get all you need as a matter of a hereditary right, a common right. You are free to do anything you want to do and you try to live a worthwhile life."

"Son," said the man, "you had breakfast this morning and you had lunch this noon before you took your walk. You'll eat dinner tonight and you'll have a drink or two. Tomorrow you'll get a new shirt or a pair of shoes and there will be some equipment that you'll need to carry on your work."

"That's right," said Craig.

"What I want to know," said the man, "is where did all that stuff come from? The shirt or the pair of shoes might have been made by someone who likes to make shirts and shoes. The food was cooked either by robots or by someone who likes to cook, and the drawing set or the typewriter or the power tools that you use might have been made by someone who likes to mess around making stuff like that. But before the typewriter was a typewriter it was metal in the ground, the food was grown, the clothes came from one of several raw materials. Tell me: Who grew the raw materials, who dug and smelted the ore?"

"I don't know," said Craig. "I never thought of that."

"We're *kept*," said the man. "Someone is keeping us. Me, I won't be kept."

He pulled in the tackle and twirled the pole to wrap the line around it.

"Sun is getting down a bit," he said. "I got to go and hoe."

"It was good talking to you," said Craig, getting up.

"Nice path over that way," said the man, pointing. "Good walking, lots of flowers and it's shaded, so it'll be nice and cool. If you go far enough, you'll reach an art gallery." He looked at Craig. "You're interested in art?"

148

"Yes," said Craig. "But I didn't know there was a gallery anywhere around."

"Well, there is," said the man. "Good paintings. Some wood statuary that is better than average. A few pieces of good jade. Go there myself when I have the time."

"Well, thanks," said Craig.

"Funny-looking building," the man said. "Group of buildings, really. Architect who designed them was crazier than a coot, but don't let it prejudice you. The stuff is really good."

"There's plenty of time," said Craig. "I'll drop in and have a look. Thanks for telling me."

The man got up and dusted off his trousers seat.

"If you're late in getting back," he said, "drop in and spend the night. My shack is just across the way. Plenty of grub and there is room for two to sleep."

"Thank you," said Craig. "I may do it."

He had no intention of accepting the offer.

The man held out his hand. "My name is Sherman," he said. "Glad you came along."

They shook hands.

Sherman went to hoe his garden and Craig walked down the path.

The buildings seemed to be quite close and yet it was hard to make out their lines. It was because of some crazy architectural principle, Craig decided. Sherman had said the architect was crazier than a coot. One time when he looked at them, they looked one way; when he looked again they were different somehow. They were never twice the same.

They were pink until he decided that they weren't pink at all, but were really blue; there were other times when they seemed neither pink nor blue, but a sort of green, although it wasn't really green.

They were beautiful, of course, but it was a disturbing beauty—a brand-new sort of beauty. Something, Craig decided, that Sherman's misplaced genius had thought up, although it did seem funny that a place like this could exist without his ever hearing about it. Still, such a thing was understandable when he remembered that everyone was so self-consciously wrapped up in his work

149

that he never paid attention to what anyone else was doing.

There was one way, of course, to find out what it was all about and that was to go and see.

The buildings, he estimated, were no more than a good five minutes' walk across a landscaped meadow that was a thing of beauty in itself.

He started out and walked for fifteen minutes, and he did not get there. It seemed, however, that he was viewing the buildings from a slightly different angle, although that was hard to tell because they refused to stay in place but seemed to be continually shifting and distorting their lines.

It was, of course, no more than an optical illusion.

He started out again.

After another fifteen minutes he was still no closer, although he could have sworn that he had kept his course headed straight toward the buildings.

It was then that he began to feel the panic.

He stood quite still and considered the situation as sanely as he could and decided there was nothing for it but to try again and this time pay strict attention to what he was doing.

He started out, moving slowly, almost counting his steps as he walked, concentrating fiercely upon keeping each step headed in the right direction.

It was then he discovered he was slipping. It appeared that he was going straight ahead but, as a matter of fact, he was slipping sidewise as he walked. It was just as if there were something smooth and slippery in front of him that translated his forward movement into a sidewise movement without his knowing it. Like a fence, a fence that he couldn't see or sense.

He stopped, and the panic that had been gnawing at him broke into cold and terrible fear.

Something flickered in front of him. For a moment it seemed that he saw an eye, one single staring eye, looking straight at him. He stood rigid, and the sense that he was being looked at grew, and now it seemed that there were strange shadows on the grass beyond the fence that was invisible. As if someone, or something, that he couldn't see was standing there and looking at him, watching with amusement his efforts to walk through the fence.

150

He lifted a hand and thrust it out in front of him and there was no fence, but his hand and arm slipped sidewise and did not go forward more than a foot or so.

He felt the kindness, then, the kindness and the pity and the vast superiority.

And he turned and fled.

He hammered on the door, and Sherman opened it.

Craig stumbled in and fell into a chair. He looked up at the man he had talked with that afternoon.

"You knew," he said. "You knew and you sent me to find out."

Sherman nodded. "You wouldn't have believed me if I'd told you."

"What are they?" asked Craig, his words tumbling wildly. "What are they doing there?"

"I don't know what they are," said Sherman.

He walked to the stove and took a lid off a kettle and looked at what was cooking. Whatever it was, it had a hungry smell. Then he walked to the table and took the chimney off an antique oil lamp, struck a match and lit it.

"I go it simple," he said. "No electricity. No nothing. I hope that you don't mind. Rabbit stew for supper."

He looked at Craig across the smoking lamp, and in the flickering light it seemed that his head floated in the air, for the glow of the lamp blotted out his body.

"But what are *they?*" demanded Craig. "What kind of fence is that? What are they fenced in for?"

"Son," said Sherman, "they aren't the ones who are fenced in."

"They aren't . . ."

"It's us," said Sherman. "Can't you see it? *We* are the ones who are fenced in."

"You said this afternoon," said Craig, "that we were kept. You mean they're keeping us?"

Sherman nodded. "That's the way I have it figured. They're keeping us, watching over us, taking care of us. There's nothing that we want that we can't have for the simple asking. They're taking real good care of us."

"But why?"

"I don't know," said Sherman. "A zoo, maybe. A

reservation, maybe. A place to preserve the last of a species. They don't mean us any harm."

"I know they don't," said Craig. "I felt them. That's what frightened me."

He sat in silence of the shack and smelled the cooking rabbit and watched the flicker of the lamp.

"What can we do about it?" he asked.

"That's the thing," said Sherman, "that we have to figure out. Maybe we don't want to do anything at all."

Sherman went to the stove and stirred the rabbit stew.

"You are not the first," he said, "and you will not be the last. There were others before you and there will be others like you who'll come along this way, walking off their troubles."

He put the lid back on the kettle.

"We're watching them," he said, "the best we can. Trying to find out. They can't keep us fooled and caged forever."

Craig sat in his chair, remembering the kindness and the pity.

SHADOW SHOW

I

BAYARD LODGE, chief of Life Team No. 3, sat at his desk and stared across it angrily at Kent Forester, the team's psychologist.

"The Play must go on," said Forester. "I can't be responsible for what might happen if we dropped it even for a night or two. It's the one thing that holds us all together. It is the unifying glue that keeps us sane and preserves our sense of humor. And it gives us something to think about."

"I know," said Lodge, "but with Henry dead . . ."

"They'll understand," Forrester promised. "I'll talk to them. I know they'll understand."

"They'll understand all right," Lodge agreed. "All of us recognize the necessity of the Play. But there is something else. One of those characters was Henry's."

Forester nodded. "I've been thinking of that, too."

"Do you know which one?"

Forester shook his head.

"I thought you might," said Lodge. "You've been beating out your brains to get them figured out, to pair up the characters with us."

Forester grinned sheepishly.

"I don't blame you," said Lodge. "I know why you're doing it."

"It would be a help," admitted Forester. "It would give me a key to every person here. Just consider—when a character went illogical . . ."

"They're all illogical," said Lodge. "That's the beauty of them."

"But the illogic runs true to a certain zany pattern," Forester pointed out. "You can use that very zaniness and set up a norm."

"You've done that?"

"Not as a graph," said Forester, "but I have it well in mind. When the illogic deviates it's not too hard to spot it."

"It's been deviating?"

Forester nodded. "Sharply at times. The problem that we have—the way that they are thinking . . ."

"Call it attitude," said Lodge.

For a moment the two of them were silent. Then Forrester asked, "Do you mind if I ask why you insist on attitude?"

"Because it is an attitude," Lodge told him. "It's an attitude conditioned by the life we lead. An attitude traceable to too much thinking, too much searching of the soul. It's an emotional thing, almost a religious thing. There's little of the intellectual in it. We're shut up too tightly. Guarded too closely. The importance of our work is stressed too much. We aren't normal humans. We're off balance all the time. How in the world can we be normal humans when we lead no normal life?"

"It's a terrible responsibility," said Forester. "They face it each day of their lives."

"The responsibility is not theirs."

"Only if you agree that the individual counts for less than the race. Perhaps not even then, for there are definite racial implications in this project, implications that can become terribly personal. Imagine making—"

"I know," said Lodge impatiently. "I've heard it from every one of them. Imagine making a human being not in the image of humanity."

"And yet it would be human," Forester said. "That is the point, Bayard. Not that we would be manufacturing life, but that it would be human life in the shape of monsters. You wake up screaming, dreaming of those monsters. A monster itself would not be bad at all, if it were no more than a monster. After centuries of traveling to the stars, we are used to monsters."

Lodge cut him off. "Let's get back to the Play."

"We'll have to go ahead," insisted Forester.

"There'll be one character missing," Lodge warned him. "You know what that might do. It might throw the entire thing off balance, reduce it to confusion. That would be worse than no Play at all. Why can't we wait a few days and start over, new again? With a new Play, a new set of characters."

"We can't do that," said Forester, "because each of us has identified himself or herself with a certain character. That character has become a part, an individual part, of each of us. We're living split lives, Bayard. We're split personalities. We have to be to live. We have to be because not a single one of us could bear to be himself alone.

"You're trying to say that we must continue the Play as an insurance of our sanity."

"Something like that. Not so grim as you make it sound. In ordinary circumstances there'd be no question we could dispense with it. But this is no ordinary circumstance. Every one of us is nursing a guilt complex of horrendous magnitude. The Play is an emotional outlet, a letdown from the tension. It gives us something to talk about it. It keeps us from sitting around at night washing out the stains of guilt. It supplies the ridiculous in our lives—it is our daily comic strip, our chuckle or our belly laugh."

Lodge got up and paced up and down the room.

"I said attitude," he declared, "and it is an attitude—a silly, crazy attitude. There is no reason for the guilt complex. But they coddle it as if it were a thing that kept them human, as if it might be the one last identity they retain with the outside world and the rest of mankind.

They come to me and they talk about it—as if I could do something about it. As if I could throw up my hands and say, well, all right, then, let's quit. As if I didn't have a job to do.

"They say we're taking a divine power into our hands, that life came to be by some sort of godly intervention, that its blasphemous and sacrilegious for mere man to try to duplicate that feat.

"And there's an answer to that one—a logical answer, but they can't see the logic, or won't listen to it. Can Man do anything divine? If life is divine, then Man cannot create it in his laboratories no matter what he does, cannot put it on a mass production basis. If Man can create life out of his chemicals, out of his knowledge, if he can make one living cell by the virtue of his techinique and his knowledge, then that will prove divine intervention was unnecessary to the genesis of life. And if we have that proof—if we know that a divine instrumentality is unnecessary for the creation of life, doesn't that very proof and fact rob it of divinity?"

"They are seeking an escape," said Forester, trying to calm him. "Some of them may believe what they say, but there are others who are merely afraid of the responsibility—the moral responsibility. They start thinking how it would be to live with something like that the rest of their lives. You had the same situation a thousand years ago when men discovered and developed atomic fission. They did it and they shuddered. They couldn't sleep at night. They woke up screaming. They knew what they were doing—that they were unloosing terrible powers. And we know what we are doing."

Lodge went back to his desk and sat down.

"Let me think about it, Kent," he said. "You may be right. I don't know. There are so many things that I don't know."

"I'll be back," said Forester.

He closed the door quietly when he left.

II

The Play was a never-ending soap opera, the *Old Red Barn* extended to unheard reaches of the ridiculous. It

155

had a touch of Oz and a dash of alienness and it went on and on and on.

When you put a group of people on an asteroid, when you throw a space patrol around them, when you lead them to their laboratories and point out the problem to be solved, when you keep them at that problem day after endless day, you must likewise do something to preserve their sanity.

To do this there may be books and music, films, games, dancing of an evening—all the old standby entertainment values the race has used for millennia to forget its troubles.

But there comes a time when these amusements fail to serve their purpose, when they are not enough.

Then you hunt for something new and novel—and basic —for something in which each of the isolated group may participate, something with which they can establish close personal identity and lose themselves, forgetting for a time who they are and what may be their purpose.

That's where the Play came in.

In the olden days, many years before, in the cottages of Europe and the pioneer farmsteads of North America, a father would provide an evening's entertainment for his children by means of shadow pictures. He would place a lamp or candle on a table opposite a blank wall, and sitting between the lamp and wall, he would use his hands to form the shadows of rabbit and of elephant, of horse and man and bear and many other things. For an hour or more the shadow show would parade across the wall, first one and then another—rabbit nibbling clover, the elephant waving trunk and ears, the wolf howling on a hilltop. The children would sit quiet and spellbound, for these were wonderous things.

Later, with the advent of movies and of television, of the comic book and the cheap plastic dime-store toy, the shadows were no longer wondrous and were shown no longer, but that is not the point.

Take the principle of the shadow pictures, add a thousand years of know-how, and you have the Play.

Whether the long-forgotten genius who first conceived the Play had ever known of the shadow pictures is something that's not known. But the principle was there, although the approach was different in that one used his mind and thought instead of just his hands.

And instead of rabbits and elephants appearing in one-dimensional black-and-white, in the Play the characters were as varied as the human mind might make them (since the brain is more facile than the hand) and three-dimensional in full color.

The screen was a triumph in electronic engineering, with its memory banks, its rows of sonic tubes, its color selectors, ESP antennae and other gadgets, but it was the minds of the audience that did the work, supplying the raw material for the Play upon the screen. It was the audience that conceived the characters, that led them through their actions, that supplied the lines they spoke. It was the combined will of the audience that supplied the backdrops and dreamed up the properties.

At first the Play had been a haphazard thing, with the characters only half developed, playing at cross purposes, without personalities, and little more than cartoons paraded on the stage. At first the backdrops and the properties were the crazy products of many minds flying off at tangents. At times no fewer than three moons would be in the sky simultaneously, all in different phases. At times snow would be falling at one end of the stage and bright sunlight would pour down on palm trees at the other end.

But in time the Play developed. The characters grew to full stature, without missing arms and legs, acquired personalities, rounded out into full-blown living beings. The background became the result of a combined effort to achieve effective setting rather than nine different people trying desperately to fill in the blank spots.

In time direction and purpose had been achieved so that the action flowed smoothly, although there never came a time when any of the nine were sure of what would happen next.

That was the fascination of it. New situations were continually being introduced by one character or another, with the result that the human creators of the other characters were faced with the need of new lines and action to meet the changing situations.

It became in a sense of contest of wills, with each participant seeking advantages for his character, or, on the other hand, forced to backtrack to escape disaster. It became, after a time, a never-ending chess game in which each player pitted himself or herself against the other eight.

And no one knew, of course, to whom any of the characters belonged. Out of this grew up a lively guessing game and many jokes and sallies, and this was to the good, for that was what the Play was for: to lift the minds of the participants out of their daily work and worries.

Each evening after dinner the nine gathered in the theater, and the screen sprang into life and the nine characters performed their parts and spoke their lines: the Defenseless Orphan, the Mustached Villain, the Proper Young Man, the Beautiful Bitch, the Alien Monster and all the others.

Nine of them—nine men and women, and nine characters.

But now there would be only eight, for Henry Griffith had died, slumped against his bench with the notebook at his elbow.

And the Play would have to go on with one missing character—the character that had been controlled and motivated by the man who now was dead.

Lodge wondered which character would be the missing one. Not the Defenseless Orphan, certainly, for that would not have been down Henry's alley. But it might be the Proper Young Man or the Out-At-Elbows Philosopher or the Rustic Slicker.

Wait a minute there, said Lodge. Not the Rustic Slicker. The Rustic Slicker's me.

He sat idly speculating on which belonged to whom. It would be exactly like Sue Lawrence to dream up the Beautiful Bitch—a character as little like her prim, practical self as one could well imagine. He remembered that he had taunted her once concerning his suspicion and that she had been very cold to him for several days thereafter.

Forester said the Play must go on, and maybe he was right. They might adjust. God knows, they should be able to adjust to anything after participating in the Play each evening for months on end.

It was a zany thing, all right. Never getting anywhere.

Not even episodic, for it never had a chance to become episodic. Let one trend develop and some joker was sure to throw in a stumbling block that upset the trend and sent the action angling off in some new direction.

With that kind of goings-on, he thought, the disappearance of a single character shouldn't throw them off their stride.

He got up from his desk and walked to the great picture window. He stood there looking out at the bleak loneliness of the asteroid. The curved roofs of the research center fell away beneath him, shining in the starlight, to the blackness of the cragged surface. Above the jagged northern horizon lay a flush of light and in a little while it would be dawn, with the weak, watch-sized sun sailing upward to shed its feeble light upon this tiny speck of rock. He watched the flushed horizon, remembering Earth, where dawn was morning and sunset marked the beginning of the night. Here no such scheme was possible, for the days and nights were so erratic and so short that they could not be used to divide one's time. Here morning came at a certain hour, evening came at another hour, regardless of the sun, and one might sleep out a night with the sun high in the sky.

It would have been different, he thought, if we could have stayed on Earth, for there we would have had normal human contacts. We would not have thought so much or brooded; we could have rubbed away the guilt on the hides of other people.

But normal human contacts would have meant the start of rumors, would have encouraged leaks, and in a thing of this sort there could be no leaks.

For if the people of the Earth knew what they were doing, or, more correctly, what they were trying to do, they would raise a hubbub that might result in calling off the project.

Even here, he thought—even here, there are those who have their doubts and fears.

A human being must walk upon two legs and have two arms and a pair of eyes, a brace of ears, one nose, one mouth, be not unduly hairy. He must walk; he must not hop or crawl or slither.

A perversion of the human form, they said; a scrapping of human dignity; a going-too-far, farther than Man in all his arrogance was ever meant to go.

There was a rap upon the door. Lodge turned and called, "Come in."

It was Dr. Susan Lawrence. She stood in the open doorway, a stolid, dumpy, dowdy woman with an angular face that had a set of stubbornness and of purpose in it. She did not see him for a moment and stood there, turning her head, trying to find him in the dusky room.

"Over here, Sue," he called.

She closed the door and crossed the room, and stood by his side looking out the window.

Finally she said, "There was nothing wrong with him, Bayard. Nothing organically wrong. I wonder . . ."

She stood there, silent, and Lodge could feel the practical bleakness of her thoughts.

"It's bad enough," she said, "when they die and you know what killed them. It's not so bad to lose them if you've had a fighting chance to save them. But this is different. He just toppled over. He was dead before he hit the bench."

"You've examined him?"

She nodded. "I put him in the analyzers. I've got three reels of stuff. I'll check it all—later. But I'll swear there was nothing wrong."

She reached out a hand and put it on his arm, her pudgy fingers tightening.

"He didn't want to live," she said. "He was afraid to live. He thought he was close to finding something and he was afraid to find it."

"We have to find it, Sue."

"For what?" she asked. "So we can fashion humans to live on planets where humans in their present form wouldn't have a chance. So we can take a human mind and spirit and enclose it in a monster's body, hating itself. . . ."

"It wouldn't hate itself," Lodge told her. "You're thinking in anthropomorphic terms. A thing is never ugly to itself because it knows itself. Have we any proof that bipedal man is any happier than an insect or a toad?"

"But why?" she persisted. "We do not need those planets. We have more now than we can colonize. Enough Earth-type planets to last for centuries. We'll be lucky if we even colonize them all, let alone develop them, in the next five hundred years."

"We can't take the chance," he said. "We must take control while we have the chance. It was all right when we were safe and snug on Earth, but that is true no longer. We've gone out to the stars. Somewhere in the universe there are other intelligences. There have to be. Eventually we'll meet. We must be in a strong position."

"And to get into that strong position we plant colonies of human monsters. I know, Bayard—it's clever. We can design the bodies, the flesh and nerves and muscles, the organs of communication—all designed to exist upon a planet where a normal human could not live a minute. We are clever, all right, and very good technicians, but we can't breathe the life into them. There's more to life than just the colloidal combination of certain elements. There's something else, and we'll never get it."

"We will try," said Lodge.

"You'll drive good technicians out of their sanity," she said. "You'll kill some of them—not with your hands, but with your insistence. You'll keep them cooped up for years and you'll give them a Play so they'll last the longer—but you won't find life, for life is not Man's secret."

"Want to bet?" he asked, laughing at her fury.

She swung around and faced him.

"There are times," she said, "when I regret my oath. A little cyanide. . . ."

He caught her by the arm and walked her to the desk. "Let's have a drink," he said. "You can kill me later."

III

They dressed for dinner.

That was a rule. They always dressed for dinner.

It was, like the Play, one of the many little habits that they cultivated to retain their sanity, not to forget that they were a cultured people as well as ruthless seekers after knowledge—a knowledge that any one of them would have happily forsworn.

They laid aside their scalpels and their other tools, they boxed their microscopes, they ranged the culture bottles neatly in place, they put the pans of saline solu-

161

tions and their varying contents carefully away. They took their aprons off and went out and shut the door. And for a few hours they forgot, or tried to forget, who they were and what their labors were.

They dressed for dinner and assembled in the so-called drawing room for cocktails and then went in to dinner, pretending that they were no more than normal human beings—and no less.

The table was set with exquisite china and fragile glass, and there were flowers and flaming tapers. They began with an entree and their meal was served in courses by accomplished robots, and they ended with cheese and fruit and brandy and there were cigars for those who wanted them.

Lodge sat at the table's head and looked down the table at them and for a moment saw Sue Lawrence looking back at him and wondered if she were scowling or if the seeming scowl was no more than the play of candle-light upon her face.

They talked as they always talked at dinner—the inconsequential social chatter of people without worry and with little purpose. For this was the moment of forgetting and escape. This was the hour to wash away the guilt and to ignore the stain.

But tonight, he noticed, they could not pull themselves away entirely from the happenings of the day—for there was talk of Henry Griffith and of his sudden dying and they spoke of him in soft tones and with strained and sober faces. Henry had been too intense and too strange a man for anyone to know him well, but they held him in high regard, and although the robots had been careful to arrange the seating so his absence left no gap, there was a real and present sense that one of them was missing.

Chester Sifford said to Lodge, "We'll be sending Henry back?"

Lodge nodded. "We'll call in one of the patrol and it'll take him back to Earth. We'll have a short service for him here."

"But who?"

"Craven, more than likely. He was closer to Henry than any of the rest. I spoke to him about it. He agreed to say a word or two."

"Is there anyone on Earth? Henry never talked a lot."

"Some nephews and nieces. Maybe a brother or a sister. That would be all, I think."

Hugh Maitland said, "I understand we'll continue with the Play."

"That's right," Lodge told him. "Kent recommended it and I agreed. Kent knows what's best for us."

Sifford agreed. "That's his job. He's a good man at it."

"I think so, too," said Maitland. "Most psych-men stand outside the group. Posing as your conscience. But Kent doesn't work that way."

"He's a chaplain," Sifford said. "Just a goddamn chaplain."

Helen Gray sat to the left, and Lodge saw that she was not talking with anyone but only staring at the bowl of roses which this night served as a centerpiece.

Tough on her, he thought. For she had been the one who had found Henry dead and, thinking that he was merely sleeping, had taken him by the shoulder and shaken him to wake him.

Down at the other end of the table, sitting next to Forester, Alice Page was talking far too much, much more than she had ever talked before, for she was a strangely reserved woman, with a quiet beauty that had a touch of darkness in it. Now she leaned toward Forester, talking tensely, as if she might be arguing in a low tone so the others would not hear her, with Forester listening, his face masked with patience against a feeling of alarm.

They are upset, thought Lodge—far more than I had suspected. Upset and edgy, ready to explode.

Henry's death had hit them harder than he knew.

Not a lovable man, Henry still had been one of them. One of them, he thought. Why not one of us? But that was the way it always was—unlike Forester, who did his best work by being one of them, he must stand to one side, must keep intact that slight, cold margin of reserve which was all that preserved against an incident of crisis the authority which was essential to his job.

Sifford said, "Henry was close to something."

"So Sue told me."

"He was writing up his notes when he died," said Sifford. "It may be. . . ."

"We'll have a look at them," Lodge promised. "All of us together. In a day or two."

Maitland shook his head. "We'll never find it, Bayard. Not the way we're working. Not in the direction we are working. We have to take a new approach."

Sifford bristled. "What kind of approach?"

"I don't know," said Maitland. "If I knew. . . ."

"Gentlemen," said Lodge.

"Sorry," Sifford said. "I'm a little jumpy."

Lodge remembered Dr. Susan Lawrence, standing with him, looking out the window at the bleakness of the tumbling hunk of rock on which they lived and saying, "He didn't want to live. He was afraid to live."

What had she been trying to tell him? That Henry Griffith had died of intellectual fear? That he had died because he was afraid to live?

Would it actually be possible for a psychosomatic syndrome to kill a man?

IV

You could feel the tension in the room when they went to the theater, although they did their best to mask the tension. They chatted and pretended to be light-hearted, and Maitland tried a joke which fell flat upon its face and died, squirming beneath the insincerity of the laughter that its telling had called forth.

Kent was wrong, Lodge told himself, feeling a wave of terror washing over him. This business was loaded with deadly psychological dynamite. It would not take much to trigger it and it could set off a chain reaction that could wash up the team.

And if the team were wrecked the work of years was gone—the long years of education, the necessary months to get them working together, the constant, never-ending battle to keep them happy and from one another's throats. Gone would be the team confidence which over many months had replaced individual confidence and doubt, gone would be the smooth co-operation and co-ordination which worked like meshing gears, gone would be a vast percentage of the actual work they'd done, for no other team, no matter how capable it might be, could take up where another team left off, even with the notes of the first team to guide them on their way.

The curving screen covered one end of the room, sunken into the wall, with the flare of the narrow stage in front of it.

Back of that, thought Lodge, the tubes and generators, the sonics and computers—mechanical magic which turned human thought and will into the moving images that would parade across the screen. Puppets, he thought —puppets of the human mind, but with a strange and startling humanity about them that could not be achieved by carven hunks of wood.

And the difference, of course, was the difference between the mind and hand, for no knife, no matter how sharp, guided by no matter how talented and artistic a hand, could carve a dummy with half the precision or fidelity with which the mind could shape a human creature.

First, Man had created with hands alone, chipping the flint, carving out the bow and dish; then he achieved machines which were extensions of his hands and they turned out artifacts which the hands alone were incapable of making; and now, Man created not with his hands nor with extensions of his hands, but with his mind and extensions of his mind, although he still must use machinery to translate and project the labor of his brain.

Someday, he thought, it will be mind alone, without the aid of machines, without the help of hands.

The screen flickered and there was a tree upon it, then another tree, a bench, a duck pond, grass, a distant statue, and behind it all the dim, tree-broken outlines of city towers.

That was where they had left it the night before, with the cast of characters embarked upon a picnic in a city park—a picnic that was almost certain to remain a picnic for mere moments only before someone should turn it into something else.

Tonight, he hoped, they'd let it stay a picnic, let it run its course, take it easy for a change, not try any fancy stuff—for tonight, of all nights, there must be no sudden jolts, no terrifying turns. A mind forced to guide its character through the intricacies of a suddenly changed plot

165

or some outlandish situation might crack beneath the effort.

As it was, there'd be one missing character and much would depend upon which one it was.

The scene stood empty, like a delicate painting of a park in springtime with each thing fixed in place.

Why were they waiting? What were they waiting for?

They had set the stage. What were they waiting for?

Someone thought of a breeze and you could hear the whisper of it, moving in the trees, ruffling the pond.

Lodge brought his character into mind and walked him on the stage, imagining his gangling walk, the grass stem stuck in his mouth, the curl of unbarbered hair above his collar.

Someone had to start it off. Someone—

The Rustic Slicker turned and hustled back off stage. He hustled back again, carrying a great hamper. "Forgot m' basket," he said, with rural sheepishness.

Someone tittered in the darkened room.

Thank God for that titter! It is going all right. *Come on, the rest of you!*

The Out-At-Elbows Philosopher strode on stage. He was a charming fellow, with no good intent at all—a cadger, a bum, a fullfledged fourflusher behind the façade of his flowered waistcoat, the senatorial bearing, the long, white, curling locks.

"My friend," he said. "My friend."

"Y' ain't m' friend," the Rustic Slicker told him, "till y' pay me back m' three hundred bucks."

Come on, the rest of you!

The Beautiful Bitch showed up with the Proper Young Man, who any moment now was about to get dreadfully disillusioned.

The Rustic Slicker had squatted on the grass and opened his hamper. He began to take out stuff—a ham, a turkey, a cheese, a vacuum jug, a bowl of Jello, a tin of kippered herring.

The Beautiful Bitch made exaggerated eyes at him and wiggled her hips. The Rustic Slicker blushed, ducking his head.

Kent yelled from the audience: "Go ahead and ruin him!"

Everyone laughed.

It was going to be all right. It would be all right.

Get the audience and the players kidding back and forth and it was bound to be all right.

"Ah think that's a good idee, honey," said the Beautiful Bitch. "Ah do believe Ah will."

She advanced upon the Slicker.

The Slicker, with his head still ducked, kept on taking things out of the hamper—more by far than could have been held in any ten such hampers.

He took out rings of bologna, stacks of wieners, mounds of marshmallows, a roast goose—and a diamond necklace.

The Beautiful Bitch pounced on the necklace, shrieking with delight.

The Out-At-Elbows Philosopher had jerked a leg off the turkey and was eating it, waving it between bites to emphasize the flowery oration he had launched upon.

"My friends—" he orated between bites—"my friends, in this vernal season it is right and proper, I said right and proper, sir, that a group of friends should forgather to commune with nature in her gayest aspects, finding retreat such as this even in the heart of a heartless city . . ."

He would go on like that for hours unless something intervened to stop him. The situation being as it was, something was almost bound to stop him.

Someone had put a sportive, if miniature, whale into the pond, and the whale, acting much more like a porpoise than a whale, was leaping about in graceful curves and scaring the hell out of the flock of ducks which resided on the pond.

The Alien Monster sneaked in and hid behind a tree. You could see with half an eye that he was bent upon no good.

"Watch out!" yelled someone in the audience, but the actors paid no attention to the warning. There were times when they could be incredibly stupid.

The Defenseless Orphan came on stage on the arm of the Mustached Villain (and there was no good intent in that situation, either) with the Extra-Terrestrial Ally trailing along behind them.

"Where is the Sweet Young Thing?" asked the Mustached Villain. "She's the only one who's missing."

"She'll be along," said the Rustic Slicker. "I saw her at the corner saloon building up a load—"

The Philosopher stopped his oration in midsentence, halted the turkey drumstick in midair. His silver mane did its best to bristle, and he whirled upon the Rustic Slicker.

"You are a cad, sir," he said, "to say a thing like that, a most contemptible cad!"

"I don't care," said the Slicker. "No matter what y' say, that's what she was doing."

"You lay off him," shrilled the Beautiful Bitch, fondling the diamond necklace. "He's mah frien' and you can't call him a cad."

"Now, B.B.," protested the Proper Young Man, "you keep out of this."

She spun on him. "You shut yoah mouth," she said. "You mealy hypocrite. Don't you tell me what to do. Too nice to call me by mah rightful name, but using just initials. You prissy-panted high-binder, don't you speak to me."

The Philosopher stepped ponderously forward, stooped down and swung his arm. The half-eaten drumstick took the Slicker squarely across the chops.

The Slicker rose slowly to his feet, one hand grasping the roast goose.

"So y' want to play," he said.

He hurled the goose at the Philosopher. It struck squarely on the flowered waistcoat. It was greasy and it splashed.

Oh, Lord, thought Lodge. Now the fat's in the fire for sure! Why did the Philosopher act the way he did? Why couldn't they have left it a simple, friendly picnic, just this once? Why did the person whose character the Philosopher was make him swing that drumstick?

And why had he, Bayard Lodge, made the Slicker throw the goose?

He went cold all over at the question, and when the answer came he felt a hand reach into his belly and start twisting at his guts.

For the answer was: He hadn't!

He hadn't made the Slicker throw the goose. He'd felt a flare of anger and a hard, cold hatred, but he had not willed his character to retaliatory action.

168

He kept watching the screen, seeing what was going on, but with only half his mind, while the other half quarreled with itself and sought an explanation.

It was the machine that was to blame—it was the machine that had made the Slicker throw the goose, for the machine would know, almost as well as a human knew, the reaction that would follow a blow upon the face. The machine had acted automatically, without waiting for the human thought. Sure, perhaps, of what the human thought would be.

It's logical, said the arguing part of his mind—it's logical that the machine would know, and logical once again that being sure of knowing, it would react automatically.

The Philosopher had stepped cautiously backward after he had struck the blow, standing at attention, presenting arms, after a manner of speaking, with the mangy drumstick.

The Beautiful Bitch clapped her hands and cried, "Now you-all got to fight a duel!"

"Precisely, miss," said the Philosopher, still stiffly at attention. "Why else do you think I struck him?"

The goose grease dripped slowly off his ornate vest, but you never would have guessed for so much as an instant that he thought he was anything but faultlessly turned out.

"But it should have been a glove," protested the Proper Young Man.

"I didn't have a glove, sir," said the Philosopher, speaking a truth that was self-evident.

"It's frightfully improper," persisted the Proper Young Man.

The Mustached Villain flipped back his coattails and reaching into his back pockets, brought out two pistols.

"I always carry them," he said with a frightful leer, "for occasions such as this."

We have to break it up, thought Lodge. We have to stop it. We can't let it go on.

He made the Rustic Slicker say, "Now lookit here, now. I don't want to fool around with firearms. Someone might get hurt."

"You have to fight," said the leering Villain, holding

both pistols in one hand and twirling his mustaches with the other.

"He has the choice of weapons," observed the Proper Young Man. "As the challenged party . . ."

The Beautiful Bitch stopped clapping her hands.

"You keep out of this," she screamed. "You sissy—you just don't want to see them fight."

The Villain bowed. "The Slicker has the choice," he said.

The Extra-Terrestrial Ally piped up. "This is ridiculous," it said. "All you humans are ridiculous."

The Alien Monster stuck his head out from behind the tree.

"Leave 'em alone," he bellowed in his frightful brogue. "If they want to fight, let 'em go ahead and fight."

Then he curled himself into a wheel by the simple procedure of putting his tail into his mouth and started to roll. He rolled around the duck pond at a fearful pace, chanting all the while: "Leave 'em fight. Leave 'em fight. Leave 'em fight." Then he popped behind his tree again.

The Defenseless Orphan complained, "I thought this was a picnic."

And so did all the rest of us, thought Lodge.

Although you could have bet, even before it started, that it wouldn't stay a picnic.

"Your choice, please," said the Villain to the Slicker, far too politely. "Pistols, knives, swords, battle axes—"

Ridiculous, thought Lodge.

Make it ridiculous.

He made the Slicker say, "Pitchforks at three paces."

The Sweet Young Thing tripped lightly on the stage. She was humming a drinking song, and you could see that she'd picked up quite a glow.

But she stopped at what she saw before her; the Philosopher dripping goose grease, the Villain clutching a pistol in each hand, the Beautiful Bitch jangling a diamond necklace, and she asked, "What is going on here?"

The Out-At-Elbows Philosopher relaxed his pose and rubbed his hands together with smirking satisfaction.

"Now," he said, oozing good fellowship and cheer, "isn't this a cozy situation. All nine of us are here—"

In the audience, Alice Page leaped to her feet, put her hands up to her face, pressed her palms tight against

170

her temples, closed her eyes quite shut and screamed and screamed and screamed.

V

There had been, not eight characters, but nine.

Henry Griffith's character had walked on with the rest of them.

"You're crazy, Bayard," Forester said. "When a man is dead, he's dead. Whether he still exists or not, I don't profess to know, but if he does exist it is not on the level of his previous existence; it is on another plane, in another state of being, in another dimension, call it what you will, religionist or spiritualist, the answer is the same."

Lodge nodded his agreement. "I was grasping at straws. Trying to dredge up every possibility. I know that Henry's dead. I know the dead stay dead. And yet, you'll have to admit, it is a natural thought. Why did Alice scream? Not because the nine characters were there. But because of why there might be nine of them. The ghost in us dies hard."

"It's not only Alice," Forester told him. "It's all the others, too. If we don't get this business under control, there'll be a flare-up. The emotional index was already stretched pretty thin when this happened—doubt over the purpose of the research, the inevitable wear and tear of nine people living together for months on end, a sort of cabin fever. It all built up. I've watched it building up and I've held my breath."

"Some joker out there subbed for Henry," Lodge said. "How does that sound to you? Someone handled his own character and Henry's, too."

"No one could handle more than one character," said Forester.

"Someone put a whale into that duck pond."

"Sure, but it didn't last long. The whale jumped a time or two and then was gone. Whoever put it there couldn't keep it there."

"We all co-operate on the setting and the props. Why couldn't someone pull quietly out of that co-operation and concentrate all his mind on two characters?"

Forester looked doubtful. "I suppose it could be done. But the second character probably would be out of whack.

171

Did you notice any of them that seemed a little strange?"

"I don't know about strange," said Lodge, "but the Alien Monster hid—"

"Henry's character wasn't the Alien Monster."

"How can you be sure?"

"Henry wasn't the kind of man to cook up an alien monster."

"All right, then. Which one is Henry's character?"

Forester slapped the arm of his chair impatiently. "I've told you, Bayard, that I don't know who any of them are. I've tried to match them up and it can't be done."

"It would help if we knew. Especially . . ."

"Especially Henry's character," said Forester. He left the chair and paced up and down the office.

"Your theory of some joker putting on Henry's character is all wrong," he said. "How would he know which one?"

Lodge raised his hand and smote the desk. "The Sweet Young Thing!" he shouted.

"What's that?"

"The Sweet Young Thing. She was the last to walk on. Don't you remember? The Mustached Villain asked where she was and the Rustic Slicker said he saw her in a saloon and—"

"Good Lord!" breathed Forester. "And the Out-At-Elbows Philosopher was at great pains to announce that all of them were there. Needling us! Jeering at us!"

"You think the Philosopher is the one, then? He's the joker. The one who produced the Sweet Young Thing— the ninth member of the cast. The ninth one to appear would have to be Henry's character, don't you see. You said yourself it couldn't be done because you wouldn't know which one it was. But you could know—you'd know when eight were on the stage that the missing one was Henry's character."

"Either there was a joker," Forester said, "or the cast itself is somehow sentient—has come half way alive."

Lodge scowled. "I can't buy that one, Kent. They're images of our minds. We call them up, we put them through their paces, we dismiss them. They depend utterly on us. They couldn't have a separate identity. They're creatures of our mind and that is all."

"It wasn't exactly along that line that I was thinking,"

said Forester. "I was thinking of the machine itself. It takes the impressions from our minds and shapes them. It translates what we think into the images on the screen. It transforms our thoughts into seeming actualities. . . ."

"A memory . . ."

"I think the machine may have a memory," Forester declared. "God knows it has enough sensitive equipment packed into it to have almost anything. The machine does more of it than we do, it contributes more than we do. After all, we're the same drab old mortals that we always were. We've just got clever, that is all. We've built extensions of ourselves. The machine is an extension of our imagery."

"I don't know," protested Lodge. "I simply do not know. This going around in circles. This incessant speculation."

But he did know, he told himself. He did know that the machine could act independently, for it had made the Slicker throw the goose. But that was different from handling a character from scratch, different from putting on a character that should not appear. It had simply been a matter of an induced, automatic action—and it didn't mean a thing.

Or did it?

"The machine could walk on Henry's character," Forester persisted. "It could have the Philosopher mock us."

"But why?" asked Lodge and even as he asked it, he knew why the machine might do just that, and the thought of it made icy worms go crawling up his back.

"To show us," Forester said, "that it was sentient, too."

"But it wouldn't do that," Lodge argued. "If it were sentient it would keep quiet about it. That would be its sole defense. We could smash it. We probably would smash it if we thought it had come alive. We could dismantle it; we could put an end to it."

He sat in the silence that fell between them and felt the dread that had settled on this place—a strange dread compounded of an intellectual and moral doubt, of a man who had fallen dead, of one character too many, of the guarded loneliness that hemmed in their lives.

"I can't think," he said. "Let's sleep on it."

"Okay," said Forester.

"A drink?"

Forester shook his head.

He's glad to drop it, too, thought Lodge. He's glad to get away.

Like a hurt animal, he thought. All of us, like hurt animals, crawling off to be alone, sick of one another, poisoned by the same faces eternally sitting across the table or meeting in the halls, of the same mouths saying the same inane phrases over and over again until, when you meet the owner of a particular mouth, you know before he says it what he is going to say.

"Good night, Bayard."

"Night, Kent. Sleep tight."

"See you."

"Sure," said Lodge.

The door shut softly.

Good night. Sleep tight. Don't let the bedbugs bite.

VI

He woke, screaming in the night.

He sat bolt upright in the middle of the bed and searched with numbed mind for the actuality, slowly, clumsily separating the actuality from the dream, becoming aware again of the room he slept in, of the furniture, of his own place and who he was and what he did and why he happened to be there.

It was all right, he told himself. It had been just a dream. The kind of dream that was common here. The kind of dream that everyone was having.

The dream of walking down a street or road, or walking up a staircase, of walking almost anywhere and of meeting something—a spiderlike thing, or a wormlike thing, or a squatting monstrosity with horns and drooling mouth or perhaps something such as could be fabricated only in a dream and have it stop and say hello and chat—for it was human, too, just the same as you.

He sat and shivered at the memory of the one he'd met, of how it had put a hairy, taloned claw around his shoulder, of how it had drooled upon him with great affection and had asked him if he had the time to catch a drink because it had a thing or two it wanted to talk

174

with him about. Its odor had been overpowering and its shape obscene, and he'd tried to shrink from it, had tried to run from it, but could neither shrink nor run, for it was a man like him, clothed in different flesh.

He swung his legs off the bed and found his slippers with searching toes and scuffed his feet into them. He found his robe and stood up and put it on and went out to the office.

There he mixed himself a drink.

Sleep tight, he thought. God, how can a man sleep tight? Now it's got me as well as all the others.

The guilt of it—the guilt of what mankind meant to do. Although, despite the guilt, there was a lot of logic in it.

There were planets upon which no human could have lived for longer than a second, because of atmospheric pressure, because of overpowering gravity, because of lack of atmosphere or poison atmosphere, or because of any one or any combination of a hundred other reasons.

And yet those planets had economic and strategic value, every one of them. Some of them had both great economic and great strategic value. And if Man were to hold the galactic empire which he was carving out against the possible appearance of some as yet unknown alien foe, he must man all economic and strategic points, must make full use of all the resources of his new empire.

For that somewhere in the galaxy there were other intelligences as yet unmet by men there could be little doubt. The sheer mathematics of pure chance said there had to be. Given an infinite space, the possibility of such an intelligence also neared infinity. Friend or foe: you couldn't know. But you couldn't take a chance. So you planned and built against the day of meeting.

And in such planning, to bypass planets of economic and strategic value was sheer insanity.

Human colonies must be planted on those planets—must be planted there and grow against the day of meeting so that their numbers and their resources and their positioning in space might be thrown into the struggle if the struggle came to be.

And if Man, in his natural form, could not exist there—why, then you changed his form. You manufactured bodies that could live there, that could fit into the planets' many weird conditions, that could live on those planets and grow and build and carry out Man's plans.

Man could build those bodies. He had the technique to compound the flesh and bone and nerve, he had the skill to duplicate the mechanisms that produced the hormones, he had ferreted out the secrets of the enzymes and the amino acids and had at his fingertips all the other know-how to construct a body—any body, not just a human body. Biological engineering had become an exact science and biological blueprints could be drawn up to meet any conceivable set of planetary conditions. Man was all set to go on his project for colonization by humans in strange nonhuman forms.

Ready except for one thing: he could make everything but life.

Now the search for life went on, a top-priority, highly classified research program carried out here and on other asteroids, with the teams of biochemists, metabolists, endocrinologists and others isolated on the tumbling slabs of rock, guarded by military patrols operating out in space, hemmed in by a million regulations and uncounted security checks.

They sought for life, working down in that puzzling gray area where nonlife was separated from life by a shadow zone and a strange unpredictability that was enough to drive one mad, working with the viruses and crystals which at one moment might be dead and the next moment half alive and no man as yet who could tell why this was or how it came about.

That there was a definite key to life, hidden somewhere against Man's searching, was a belief that never wavered in the higher echelons, but on the guarded asteroids there grew up a strange and perhaps unscientific belief that life was not a matter of fact to be pinned down by formula or equation, but rather a matter of spirit, with some shading to the supernatural—that it was not something that Man was ever meant to know, that to seek it was presumptuous and perhaps sacrilegious, that it was a tangled trap into which Man had lured himself by his madcap hunt for knowledge.

And I, thought Bayard Lodge, I am one of those who drive them on in this blind and crazy search for a thing that we were never meant to find, that for our peace of mind and for our security of soul we never should have sought. I reason with them when they whisper out their fears, I kid them out of it when they protest the inhumanity of the course we plan, I keep them working and I kill each of them just a little every day, kill the humanity of them inch by casual inch—and I wake up screaming because a *human* thing I met put its arm around me and asked me to have a drink with it.

He finished off his drink and poured another one and this time did not bother with the mix.

"Come on," he said to the monster of the dream. "Come on, friend. I'll have that drink with you."

He gulped it down and did not notice the harshness of the uncut liquor.

"Come on," he shouted at the monster. "Come on and have that drink with me!"

He stared around the room, waiting for the monster.

"What the hell," he said, "we're all human, aren't we?"

He poured another one and held it in a fist that suddenly was shaky.

"Us humans," he said, still talking to the monster, "have got to stick together."

VII

All of them met in the lounge after breakfast, and Lodge, looking from face to face, saw the terror that lay behind the masks they kept in front of them, could sense the unvoiced shrieking that lay inside of them, held imprisoned by the iron control of breeding and of discipline.

Kent Forester carefully lit a cigarette and when he spoke his voice was conversationally casual, and Lodge, watching him as he talked, knew the price he paid to keep his voice casual.

"This is something," Forester said, "that we can't allow to keep on eating on us. We have to talk it out."

"You mean rationalize it?" asked Sifford.

Forester shook his head. "Talk it out, I said. This is once we can't kid ourselves."

"There were nine characters last night," said Craven.

"And a whale," said Forester.

177

"You mean one of . . ."

"I don't know. If one of us did, let's speak up and say so. There's not a one among us who can't appreciate a joke."

"A grisly joke," said Craven.

"But a joke," said Forester.

"I would like to think it was a joke," Maitland declared. "I'd feel a lot easier if I knew it was a joke."

"That's the point," said Forester. "That's what I'm getting at."

He paused a moment. "Anyone?" he asked.

No one said a word.

They waited.

"No one, Kent," said Lodge.

"Perhaps the joker doesn't want to reveal himself," said Forester. "I think all of us could understand that. Maybe we could hand out slips of paper."

"Hand them out," Sifford grumbled.

Forester took sheets of folded paper from his pocket, carefully tore the strips. He handed out the strips.

"If anyone played a joke," Lodge pleaded, "for God's sake let us know."

The slips came back. Some of them said "no," others said "no joke," one said "I didn't do it."

Forester wadded up the strips.

"Well, that lets that idea out," he said. "I must admit I didn't have much hope."

Craven lumbered to his feet. "There's one thing that all of us have been thinking," he said, "and it might as well be spoken. It's not a pleasant subject."

He paused and looked around him at the others, as if defying them to stop him.

"No one liked Henry too well," he said. "Don't deny it. He was a hard man to like. A hard man any way you look at him. I was closer to him than any of you. I've agreed to say a few words for him at the service this afternoon. I am glad to do it, for he was a good man despite his hardness. He had a tenacity of will, a stubbornness such as you seldom find even in a hard man. And he had moral scruples that none of us could guess. He would talk to me a little—really talk—and that's something that he never did with the rest of you.

"Henry was close to something. He was scared. He died.

"There was nothing wrong with him."

Craven looked at Dr. Lawrence.

"Was there, Susan?" he asked. "Was there anything wrong with him?"

"Not a thing," said Dr. Susan Lawrence. "He should not have died."

Craven turned to Lodge. "He talked with you recently."

"A day or two ago," said Lodge. "He seemed quite normal then."

"What did he talk about?"

"Oh, the usual things. Minor matters."

"Minor matters?" Mocking.

"All right, then. If you want it that way. He talked about not wanting to go on. He said our work was unholy. That's the word he used—unholy."

Lodge looked around the room. "That's one the rest of you have never thought to use. Unholy."

"He was more insistent than usual?"

"Well, no," said Lodge. "It was the first time he had ever talked to me about it. The only person engaged in the research here, I believe, who had not talked with me about it at one time or another."

"And you talked him into going back."

"We discussed it."

"You killed the man."

"Perhaps," said Lodge. "Perhaps I'm killing all of you. Perhaps you're killing yourselves and I myself. How am I to know?"

He said to Dr. Lawrence, "Sue, could a man die of a psychosomatic illness brought about by fear?"

"Clinically, no," said Susan Lawrence. "Practically, I'm afraid, the answer might be yes."

"He was trapped," said Craven.

"Mankind's trapped," snapped Lodge. "If you must point your finger, point it at all of us. Point it at the whole community of Man."

"I don't think," Forester interrupted, "that this is pertinent."

"It is," insisted Craven, "and I will tell you why. I'd be the last to admit the existence of a ghost—"

Alice Page came swiftly to her feet. "Stop it!" she cried. "Stop it! Stop it! Stop it!"

"Miss Page, please," said Craven.

"But you're saying . . ."

"I'm saying that if there ever was a situation where a departed spirit had a motive—and I might even say a right—to come back and haunt his place of death, this is it."

"Sit down, Craven," Lodge commanded, sharply.

Craven hesitated angrily, then sat down, grumbling to himself.

Lodge said, "If there's any point in continuing the discussion along these lines, I insist that it be done objectively."

Maitland said, "There's no point to it I can see. As scientists who are most intimately concerned with life we must recognize that death is an utter ending."

"That," objected Sifford, "is open to serious question and you know it."

Forester broke in, his voice cool. "Let's defer the matter for a moment. We can come back to it. There is another thing."

He hurried on. "Another thing that we should know. Which of the characters was Henry's character?"

No one said a word.

"I don't mean," said Forester, "to try to find which belonged to whom. But by a process of elimination . . ."

"All right," said Sifford. "Hand out the slips again."

Forester brought out the paper in his pocket, tore more strips.

Craven protested. "Not just slips," he said. "I won't fall for a trick like that."

Forester looked up from the slips.

"Trick?"

"Of course," said Craven, harshly. "Don't deny it. You've been trying to find out."

"I don't deny it," Forester told him. "I'd have been derelict in my duty if I hadn't tried."

Lodge said, "I wonder why we keep this secret thing so closely to ourselves. It might be all right under normal circumstances, but these aren't normal circumstances. I think it might be best if we made a clean breast of it. I, for one, am willing. I'll lead off if you only say the word."

He waited for the word.

There was no word.

They all stared back at him and there was nothing in their faces—no anger, no fear, nothing at all that a man could read.

Lodge shrugged the defeat from his shoulders.

He said to Craven, "All right then. What were you saying?"

"I was saying that if we wrote down the names of our characters it would be no better than standing up and shouting them aloud. Forester knows our handwriting. He could spot every slip."

Forester protested. "I hadn't thought of it. I ask you to believe I hadn't. But what Craven says is true."

"All right, then?" asked Lodge.

"Ballots," Craven said. "Fix up ballots with the characters' names upon them."

"Aren't you afraid we might be able to identify your X's?"

Craven looked levelly at Lodge. "Since you mention it, I might be."

Forester said, wearily. "We have a batch of dies down in the labs. Used for stamping specimens. I think there's an X among them."

"That would satisfy you?" Lodge asked Craven.

Craven nodded that it would.

Lodge heaved himself out of the chair.

"I'll get the stamp," he said. "You can fix the ballots while I'm after it."

Children, he thought. Just so many children. Suspicious and selfish and frightened, like cornered animals. Cornered between the converging walls of fear and guilt, trapped in the corner of their own insecurity.

He walked down the stairs to the laboratories, his heels ringing on the metal treads, with the sound of his walking echoing from the hidden corners of the fear and guilt.

If Henry hadn't died right now, he thought, it might have been all right. We might have muddled through.

But he knew that probably was wrong. For if it had not been Henry's death, it would have been something else. They were ready for it—more than ready for it.

It would not have taken much at any time in the last few weeks to have lit the fuse.

He found the die and ink pad and tramped back upstairs again.

The ballots lay upon the table and someone had found a shoe box and cut a slit out of its lid to make a ballot box.

"We'll all sit over on this side of the room," said Forester, "and we'll go up, one by one, and vote."

And if anyone saw the ridiculous side of speaking of what they were about to do as voting, he pointedly ignored it.

Lodge put the die and ink pad down on the table top and walked across the room to take his seat.

"Who wants to start it off?" asked Forester.

No one said a word.

Even afraid of this, thought Lodge.

Then Maitland said he would.

They sat in utter silence as each walked forward to mark a ballot, to fold it and to drop it in the box. Each of them waited for the one to return before another walked out to the table.

Finally it was done, and Forester went to the table, took up the box and shook it, turning it this way and that to change the order of the ballots, so that no one might guess by their position to whom they might belong.

"I'll need two monitors," he said.

His eyes looked them over. "Craven," he said. "Sue."

They stood up and went forward.

Forester opened the box. He took out a ballot, unfolded it and read it, passed it on to Dr. Lawrence, and she passed it on to Craven.

"The Defenseless Orphan."

"The Rustic Slicker."

"The Alien Monster."

"The Beautiful Bitch."

"The Sweet Young Thing."

Wrong on that one, Lodge told himself. But who else could it be? She had been the last one on. She had been the ninth.

Forester went on, unfolding the ballots and reading them.

"The Extra-Terrestrial Ally."

"The Proper Young Man."

Only two left now. Only two. The Out-At-Elbows Philosopher and the Mustached Villain.

I'll make a guess, Lodge said to himself. I'll make a bet. I'll bet on which one was Henry.

He was the Mustached Villain.

Forester unfolded the last ballot and read aloud the name.

"The Mustached Villain."

So I lose the bet, thought Lodge.

He heard the rippling hiss of indrawn breath from those around him, the swift, stark terror of what the balloting had meant.

For Henry's character had been the most self-assertive and dominant in last night's Play: the Philosopher.

VIII

The script in Henry's notebook was close and crabbed, with a curtness to it, much like the man himself. His symbols and his equations were a triumph of clarity, but the written words had a curious backward, petulant slant and the phrases that he used were laconic to the point of rudeness—although whom he was being rude to, unless it were himself, was left a matter of conjecture.

Maitland closed the book with a snap and shoved it away from him, out into the center of the table.

"So that was it," he said.

They sat in quietness, their faces pale and drawn, as if in bitter fact they might have seen the ghost of Craven's hinting.

"That's the end of it," snapped Sifford. "I won't—"

"You won't what?" asked Lodge.

Sifford did not answer. He just sat there with his hands before him on the table, opening and closing them, making great tight fists of them, then straightening out his fingers, stretching them as if he meant by sheer power of will to bend them back farther than they were meant to go.

"Henry was crazy," said Susan Lawrence curtly. "A man would have to be to dream up that sort of evidence."

"As a medical person," Maitland said, "we could expect that reaction from you."

"I work with life," said Susan Lawrence. "I respect it and it is my job to preserve it as long as it can be kept within the body. I have a great compassion for the things possessing it."

"Meaning we haven't?"

"Meaning you have to live with it and come to know it for its power and greatness, for the fine thing that it is, before you can appreciate or understand its wondrous qualities."

"But, Susan—"

"And I know," she said, rushing on to head him off. "I know that it is more than decay and breakdown, more than the senility of matter. It is something greater than disease. To argue that life is the final step to which matter is reduced, the final degradation of the nobility of soil and ore and water is to argue that a static, unintelligent, purposeless existence is the norm of the universe."

"We're getting all tangled up semantically," suggested Forester. "As living things the terms we use have no comparative values with the terms that might be used for universal purpose, even if we knew those universal terms."

"Which we don't," said Helen Gray. "What you say would be true especially if what Henry had thought he had found was right."

"We'll check Henry's notes," Lodge told them grimly. "We'll follow him step by step. I think he's wrong, but on the chance he isn't, we can't pass up an angle."

Sifford bristled. "You mean even if he were right you would go ahead? That you would use even so humanly degrading a piece of evidence to achieve our purpose?"

"Of course I would," said Lodge. "If life is a disease and a senility, all right, then, it is disease and senility. As Kent and Helen pointed out, the terms are not comparative when used in a universal sense. What is poison for the universe is—well, is life for us. If Henry was right, his discovery is no more than the uncovering of a fact that has existed since time untold."

"You don't know what you're saying," Sifford said.

"But I do," Lodge told him bluntly. "You have grown neurotic. You and some of the others. Maybe I, myself. Maybe all of us. We are ruled by fear—you by the fear of your job, I by the fear that the job will not be done.

We've been penned up, we've been beating out our brains against the stone walls of our conscience and a moral value suddenly furbished up and polished until it shines like the shield of Galahad. Back on the Earth you wouldn't give this thing a second thought. You'd gulp a little, maybe, then you'd swallow it, if it were proved true, and you'd go ahead to track down that principle of decay and of disease we happen to call life. The principle itself would be only one more factor for your consideration, one more tool to work with, another bit of knowledge. But here you claw at the wall and scream."

"Bayard!" shouted Forester. "Bayard, you can't—"

"I can," Lodge told him, "and I am. I'm sick of all their whimpering and baying. I'm tired of spoonfed fanatics who drove themselves to their own fanaticism by their own synthetic fears. It takes men and women with knife-sharp minds to lick this thing we're after. It takes guts and intelligence."

Craven was white-lipped with fury. "We've worked," he shouted. "Even when everything within us, even when all our decency and intelligence and our religious instincts told us not to work, we worked. And don't say you kept us at it, you with your mealy words and your kidding and your back slapping. Don't say you laughed us into it."

Forester pounded the table with a fist. "Let's quit this arguing," he cried. "Let's get down to cases."

Craven settled back in his chair, face still white with anger. Sifford kept on making fists.

"Henry wrote a conclusion," said Forester. "Well, hardly a conclusion. Let's call it a suspicion. Now what do you want to do about it? Ignore it, run from it, test it for its proof?"

"I say, test it," Craven said. "It was Henry's work. Henry's gone and can't speak for his own beliefs. We owe at least that much to him."

"If it can be tested," Maitland qualified. "To me it sounds more like philosophy than science."

"Philosophy runs hand in hand with science," said Alice Page. "We can't simply brush it off because it sounds involved."

"I didn't say involved," Maitland objected. "What I meant was—oh, hell, let's go ahead and check it."

"Check it," Sifford said.

He swung around on Lodge. "And if it checks out, if it comes anywhere near to checking, if we can't utterly disprove it, I'm quitting. I'm serving notice now."

"That's your privilege, Sifford, any time you wish."

"It might be hard to prove anything one way or the other," said Helen Gray. "It might not be any easier to disprove than prove."

Lodge saw Sue Lawrence looking at him and there was grim laughter and something of grudging admiration and a touch of confused cynicism in her face, as if she might be saying to him, *Well, you've done it again. I didn't think you would—not this time, I didn't. But you did. Although you won't always do it. There'll come a time . . .*

"Want to bet?" he whispered at her.

She said, "Cyanide."

And although he laughed back at her, he knew that she was right—righter than she knew. For the time had already come and this was the end of Life Team No. 3.

They would go on, of course, stung by the challenge Henry Griffith had written in his notebook, still doggedly true to their training and their charge, but the heart was out of them, the fear and the prejudice too deeply ingrained within their souls, the confused tangle of their thinking too much a part of them.

If Henry Griffith had sought to sabotage the project, Lodge told himself, he had done it perfectly. In death he had done it far better than he could have, alive.

He seemed to hear in the room the dry, acerbic chuckling of the man and he wondered at the imagined chuckle, for Henry had had no humor in him.

Although Henry had been the Out-at-Elbows Philosopher and it was hard to think of Henry as that sort of character—an old humbug who hid behind a polished manner and a golden tongue. For there was nothing of the humbug in Henry, either, and his manner was not polished nor did he have the golden gift of words. He slouched and he rarely talked, and when he did he growled.

A joker, Lodge thought—had he been, after all, a joker?

Could he have used the Philosopher to lampoon the

rest of them, a character who derided them and they not knowing it?

He shook his head, arguing with himself.

If the Philosopher had kidded them, it had been gentle kidding, so gentle that none of them had known it was going on, so subtle that it had slid off them without notice.

But that wasn't the terrifying aspect of it—that Henry might have been quietly making fun of them. The terrifying thing was that the Philosopher had been second on the stage. He had followed the Rustic Slicker and during the whole time had been much in evidence— munching on the turkey leg and waving it to emphasize the running fire of pompous talk that had never slacked. The Philosopher had been, in fact, the most prominent player in the entire Play.

And that meant that no one could have put him on the stage, for no one, in the first place, could have known so soon which of the nine was Henry's character, and no one, not having handled him before, could have put the Philosopher so realistically through his paces. And none of those who had sent on their characters early in the Play could have handled two characters convincingly for any length of time—especially when the Philosopher had talked all the blessed time.

And that would cancel out at least four of those sitting in the room.

Which could mean:

That there was a ghost.

Or that the machine itself retained a memory.

Or that the eight of them had suffered mass hullucination.

He considered that last alternative and it wilted in the middle. So did the other two. None of the three made sense. Not any of it made sense—none of it at all.

Take a team of trained men and women, trained objectively, trained to look for facts, conditioned to skepticism and impatience of anything outside the pale of fact: What did it take to wreck a team like that? Not simply the cabin fever of a lonely asteroid. Not simply the nagging of awakened conscience against well established ethics. Not the atavistic, Transylvanian fear of ghosts.

187

There was some other factor. Another factor that had not been thought of yet—like the new approach that Maitland had talked about at dinner, saying they would have to take a new direction to uncover the secret that they sought. We're going at it wrong. Maitland had said. We'll have to find a new approach.

And Maitland had meant, without saying so, that in their research the old methods of ferreting out the facts were no longer valid, that the scientific mind had operated for so long in the one worn groove that it knew no other, that they must seek some fresh concept to arrive at the fact of life.

Had Henry, Lodge wondered, supplied that fresh approach? And in the supplying of it and in dying, wrecked the team as well?

Or was there another factor, as Maitland had said there must be a new approach—a factor that did not fit in with conventional thinking or standard psychology?

The Play, he wondered. Was the Play a factor? Had the Play, designed to keep the team intact and sane, somehow turned into a two-edged sword?

They were rising from the table now, ready to leave, ready to go to their rooms and to dress for dinner. And after dinner, there would be the Play again.

Habit, Lodge thought. Even with the whole thing gone to pot, they still conformed to habit.

They would dress for dinner; they would stage the Play. They would go back tomorrow morning to their workrooms and they'd work again, but the work would be a futile work, for the dedicated purpose of their calling had been burned out of them by fear, by the conflict of their souls, by death, by ghosts.

Someone touched his elbow and he saw that Forester stood beside him.

"Well, Kent?"

"How do you feel?"

"Okay," said Lodge. Then he said, "You know, of course, it's over."

"We'll try again," said Forester.

Lodge shook his head. "Not me. You, maybe. You're a younger man than I. I'm burned out too."

The Play started in where it had left off the night before, with the Sweet Young Thing coming on the stage and all the others, there, with the Out-At-Elbows Philosopher rubbing his hands together smugly and saying, "Now this is a cozy situation. All of us are here."

Sweet Young Thing (*tripping lightly*): Why, Philosopher, I know that I am late, but what a thing to say. Of course we all are here. I was unavoidably detained.

Rustic Slicker (*speaking aside, with a rural leer*): By a Tom Collins and a slot machine.

Alien Monster (*sticking out its head from behind the tree*): Tsk hrstlgn vglater, tsk . . .

And there was something wrong, Lodge told himself.

There was a certain mechanical wrongness, something out of place, a horrifying alienness that sent a shiver through you even when you couldn't spot the alienness.

There was something wrong with the Philosopher, and the wrongness was not that he should not be there, but something else entirely. There was a wrongness about the Sweet Young Thing and the Proper Young Man and the Beautiful Bitch and all the others.

There was a great deal wrong with the Rustic Slicker, and he, Bayard Lodge, knew the Rustic Slicker as he knew no other man—knew the blood and guts and brains of him, knew his thoughts and dreams and his hidden yearnings, his clodhopperish conceit, his smart-aleck snicker, the burning inferiority complex that drove him to social exhibitionism.

He knew him as every member of the audience must know his own character, as something more than an imagined person, as someone than another person, something more than friend. For the bond was strong—the bond of the created and creator.

And tonight the Rustic Slicker had drawn a little way apart, had cut the apron strings, had stood on his own with the first dawning of independence.

The Philosopher was saying: "It's quite natural that I should have commented on all of us being here. For one of us is dead. . . ."

There was no gasp from the audience, no hiss of indrawn breath, no stir, but you could feel the tension snap tight like a whining violin string.

"We have been consciences," said the Mustached Villain. "Projected conscience playing out our parts. . . ."

The Rustic Slicker said: "The consciences of mankind."

Lodge half rose out of his chair.

I didn't make him say that! I didn't want him to say that. I thought it, that was all. So help me God, I just thought it, that was all!

And now he knew what was wrong. At last, he knew the strangeness of the characters this night.

They weren't on the screen at all! They were on the stage, the little width of stage which ran before the screen!

They were no longer projected imaginations—they were flesh and blood. They were mental puppets came to sudden life.

He sat there, cold at the thought of it—cold and rigid in the quickening knowledge that by the power of mind alone—by the power of mind and electronic mysteries, Man had created life.

A new approach, Maitland had said.

Oh, Lord! A new approach!

They had failed at their work and triumphed in their play, and there'd be no longer any need of life teams, grubbing down into that gray area where life and death were interchangeable. To make a human monster you'd sit before a screen and you'd dream him up, bone by bone, hair by hair, brains, innards, special abilities and all. There'd be monsters by the billions to plant on those other planets. And the monsters would be human, for they'd be dreamed by brother humans working from a blueprint.

In just a little while the characters would step down off the stage and would mingle with them. And their creators? What would their creators do? Go screaming, raving mad?

What would he say to the Rustic Slicker?

What *could* he say to the Rustic Slicker?

And, more to the point, what would the Rustic Slicker have to say to him?

He sat, unable to move, unable to say a word or cry out a warning, waiting for the moment when they would step down.

You will also enjoy these other outstanding

BERKLEY
SCIENCE FICTION TITLES